'I'm sorry about what happened the other night... Well, not for what happened, but the fact that it happened... Well, not even that, if I'm honest, but the fact that I've been like a bear with a sore head and avoiding you... Well, we've been avoiding each other...'

Oh, for heaven's sake! Why on earth was he rambling like this? He hadn't been this incoherent even when he'd been a tongue-tied teenager asking for his first date.

He snatched a steadying breath and forced himself to meet her eyes, suddenly struck by the fact that it almost looked as if she was about to cry.

'I'm pregnant,' she whispered through trembling lips, and turned the piece of paper she held so that it faced him.

Dear Reader

Being one of a large family can be great fun, but being the eldest has its own problems—not least the fact that you're always being told you have to set a good example.

In David ffrench's case, with doting parents and a younger sister who idolised him, that was hardly a problem. Ever since he could remember everything had come to him easily: study, sport, friendship and love.

Unfortunately, he'd never needed to learn how to cope with failure or disappointment, and when both struck at his idyllically happy life he found it hard to come to terms with the loss of everything he'd cherished. Determined he wasn't going to give life the chance to hurt him again, he decided to dedicate himself totally to his absorbing career.

But he'd reckoned without meeting Leah Dawson.

Keenly intelligent and beautiful, Leah was every bit as dedicated as he was—both to her work and to avoiding relationships with the opposite sex. Neither of them had realised that their solitary, well-ordered lives would suddenly seem more like loneliness. Nor had they counted on the sparks that they would ignite in each other.

I hope you enjoy getting to know David and Leah as they struggle to heal the scars from the past so that they can become the supportive partner each of them needs.

Happy reading!

Josie

HIS UNEXPECTED CHILD

BY

JOSIE METCALFE

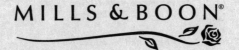

MILLS & BOON®

*First published in Great Britain 2005
Harlequin Mills & Boon Limited,
Eton House, 18-24 Paradise Road, Richmond, Surrey TW9 1SR*

© Josie Metcalfe 2005

ISBN 0 263 84322 X

*Set in Times Roman 10½ on 12 pt.
03-0805-48982*

*Printed and bound in Spain
by Litografía Rosés, S.A., Barcelona*

CHAPTER ONE

LEAH'S hand was shaking violently as she tried to put the telephone back on its cradle and she was only successful on the second attempt.

For just a moment she was blazingly angry that she'd been treated so cavalierly, but then her brain returned to its usual logical processes.

Still, she was sorely tempted to drop her head to the desk and howl her disappointment but the last thing she wanted was for the whole department to know what had just happened—at least, not until she'd had time to come to terms with it.

For a moment she glanced around the cramped room, focusing on all the things she hated about it— the shabby, boring paintwork, the limp, sun-bleached curtains and the institutional furniture piled high with the overflow of case files—and mourned the fact that she wouldn't have time to finish her self-imposed task of rearranging the chaotic filing system into something more streamlined and efficient.

'Problem?' queried a voice from the doorway, and she realised that her trembling hands could not have been the only outward sign of her feelings. She drew in a swift bracing breath before she turned to face the department's most senior nurse, knowing that the time for licking her wounds was already over.

'No problem that I know of, Kelly,' she said brightly, hoping her smile didn't look as false as it felt.

'So you got the lab results at last!' A smile lit her gamine face as she entered the room eagerly.

Lab results? Leah blinked, having to force her mind back to her first phone call of the recent session, the one before disappointment had descended over her.

'Ah... Yes! Here they are. I got Stanley to read them out for me over the phone and jotted them down.' She handed the piece of paper to Kelly. 'They've promised to follow up with written confirmation, a.s.a.p., and *I* promised to come up there personally and extract them with the most painful methods at my disposal if they didn't keep *their* promise!'

Kelly laughed at the empty threat. They both knew exactly how important it was that the labs were meticulous, especially in the work of this department, and Stanley was one of the best.

'Well, we'll see what happens, won't we,' Kelly said with a doubting shake of her dark head. 'They promised me the same, hours ago, and nothing happened. Still, I'm not the head of St Luke's Assisted Reproduction department, so perhaps that'll make all the difference.'

A swift pang of renewed disappointment tightened around Leah's heart, but she couldn't avoid breaking the news any longer. Soon everyone would know.

'Only *acting* head,' she reminded Kelly, hoping she didn't sound as bitter as she felt. She'd been carrying the full load for months while Donald had avoided coming to terms with his need for heart-bypass surgery. Due to her willingness to work herself to a standstill, her superior's sudden death had hardly registered in the smooth running of the department, and she'd hoped that it would be little more than a formality for her unofficial position as head of the AR department to be given the stamp of approval.

'That's just administrative claptrap,' Kelly declared supportively. 'We all know you're the best one for the position, especially as you've been doing it for so many weeks—'

'Apparently, not everyone agrees with you, Kelly,' Leah interrupted, her voice a little sharper than usual with restrained emotion. 'The board has appointed a new head of department from outside the hospital. He's supposed to be joining us in a matter of days.'

'Oh, Leah,' Kelly murmured, clearly stricken. At least that was some kind of sop to Leah's ego. 'Oh, damn, I'm sorry. Why didn't you say something? When did you find out?'

'Just a moment ago.' She gestured towards the phone. 'Apparently someone was supposed to have informed me of the board's decision before the weekend, but in the excitement of snagging someone as eminent as David ffrench...' She shrugged, trying to appear philosophical about hospital management's total lack of courtesy.

'David ffrench?' Kelly frowned.

'The name doesn't ring a bell with me either,' Leah agreed. 'But, then, I just grabbed the minimum time necessary from the department to attend the interview. There just wasn't time to hang around to meet the competition so I don't even know where he's been working.'

'Well, if he's such hot stuff, how come he's free to take up a position here at the drop of a hat?' Kelly demanded.

'All I know is that he's apparently been at a top-flight IVF centre in New Zealand and he's come to Britain for family reasons.'

'Is he a New Zealander?' There was a definite spark of interest in Kelly's dark eyes and Leah actually had to subdue a grin at the predictability of her colleague's reaction. 'Oh, tell me he's one of those gorgeous seven-foot rugby-playing Maoris, please! That's what this department could do with—a few really sexy hunky single men!'

'Sorry I can't oblige,' said a dry voice behind them, and they both whirled in surprise to face the man who had arrived unannounced at the office doorway. 'I'm not a New Zealander and it's years since I played any rugby.'

That didn't mean he was lacking in the looks department, Leah registered with an unexpected surge of awareness, something that hadn't happened since…for ever.

At five feet seven, she wasn't short, but she had to look up some way to meet his uncomfortably direct greeny blue gaze, in spite of the fact that she hadn't had time to change out of her heeled shoes this morning. His bronzed skin was a testament to the fact that he'd just returned from a summer in New Zealand but his face was all planes and angles as though he'd recently lost more weight than was good for him. He certainly didn't look as though he was carrying enough muscle bulk to be a rugby player now.

'You're English!' Kelly's gurgle of laughter startled her and Leah felt a wash of heat surge up into her cheeks. Had she really been standing there admiring the man's physique, for heaven's sake? Had he noticed?

'Through and through,' their new boss agreed with

a slight smile, but Leah noted that, for all his pleasant manner, the smile hadn't reached his eyes. 'In fact, I did part of my training at this very hospital.'

And *that* would account for his appointment, Leah thought waspishly, then had to stifle a grimace.

She knew she was being illogical. No hospital would appoint a head of department without being certain that they were the best for the position, especially when they had several to choose from. She would just have to learn to console herself with the idea that it had probably been her age—or lack of it—and a lack of seniority in this particular discipline that had lost her the headship this time. David ffrench looked to be several years older at least, and had already headed a similar department in New Zealand. Added to that, her experience of holding the department together over the last few months had gone largely unnoticed by the hospital hierarchy as her head of department had been covering his tracks to conceal how badly his health had been hampering him. While the extra burden had been exhausting, Leah hadn't really blamed Donald for wanting to hang on to the job he loved as long as possible. She knew what it was like to build your whole life around a special profession.

'I'm Kelly Argent,' Kelly was saying with the sort of blinding smile that would tell even the slowest-witted man that she was interested. 'I'm Senior Sister in the department.'

'David ffrench,' he said, accepting her handshake but, as far as Leah could tell, not even registering any other offers. 'I'm not actually starting till the beginning of next week but I was hoping to meet up with my second in command so that we could compare notes about the department and the case load. Is he here at the moment?'

'He?' Leah repeated in shock, her thoughts a whirling maelstrom. Had she lost out completely? Had she been so shocked by the announcement of his appointment over her that she'd missed a vital second part to that phone call? Had there been *another* appointment, replacing her without her knowledge? Was she now relegated to third in the pecking order, or even bounced out of the department altogether?

'Lee Dawson,' he said with a hint of impatience. 'The chap who's been holding everything together since my predecessor—'

'Lee!' Kelly giggled, clearly delighted with his mistake. 'You mean Leah!' She sketched a sweeping gesture in her direction. 'And I bet the panel didn't tell you that if it weren't for her working twenty-six hours a day, there wouldn't be a department for you to take charge of.'

Leah cringed with embarrassment when he turned the full force of those striking eyes on her. It had been for the sake of her—*their*—patients that she'd worked so long and hard, not to have fulsome praise heaped on her shoulders. She would far rather have had the position of head of department instead.

'Loyal staff,' her new boss said quietly, his eyes giving nothing away. 'That speaks well of a department. I hope I can earn the same sort of loyalty as my predecessor.'

'Oh, *he* wasn't the one—' Kelly began, but Leah quelled her with a glare. She might be disappointed to have lost the plum job but there was no way she wanted to start off a new working relationship with the rest of the staff taking sides.

A frown briefly pleated the smooth skin of his forehead, as though he'd suddenly become aware of unanticipated undercurrents, but with her deliberately noncommittal expression, Leah hoped that there was nothing for him to glean.

'Well, then, Leah, if it's convenient, I'd like to spend some time in the department today to see how things are run at the moment. I expect you've got everything ready for my arrival on Monday, but have you got time this morning to go over the current patient files?'

To see how things are run at the moment? Leah's heart sank. That certainly sounded as if he intended making changes before he'd even seen how things were organised. Not that there weren't changes that she'd had in mind should she have been given the job, but she already knew what needed changing because she'd been running the department for months.

'Actually, there's *nothing* ready for your arrival on Monday because we had no idea that you were coming,' she said bluntly, unable to stop her frustration coating her words. 'In fact, we'd never even heard of you until five minutes before you turned up, and we certainly didn't know that you'd been appointed head of department.'

To say that he looked taken aback was putting it mildly, Leah thought, and, in spite of her own feelings of disappointment, she suddenly found herself having to fight laughter. Was it hysteria? Perhaps. But it certainly wasn't a good example of professional courtesy, especially when she was going to have to work with the man.

'Of course, the patients' notes are completely up to date,' she assured him with a touch of justifiable pride.

He obviously didn't think so and she could hardly blame him, given the fact that there were piles of files dotted around as a result of her ongoing reorganisation. 'And the computer system the hospital uses is very quick to master so you shouldn't have any trouble accessing any other details you may need.'

'I see.' He was silent for a nerve-stretching moment as his eyes roved the apparent chaos surrounding them, the dubious expression on his face saying everything. 'And *will* you have any time free this morning?'

There was something in the tone of his voice that she couldn't put her finger on, but it made Leah feel uncomfortable. She had no idea whether he was pleased to hear that all the paperwork was in order or whether he seriously doubted it and was wondering how soon he could find a way to replace her.

Just the thought of having to leave her beloved department was enough to send a chill down her spine and she instantly resolved to be less prickly. After all, she may have applied for the post but she hadn't got it. It certainly wasn't the first disappointment she'd suffered. Life went on.

She slid back behind the desk, leaning forward to press a combination of keys on the computer keyboard until the relevant diary page flashed up onto the screen. She always arrived at least an hour before she was due to start and she may as well get their initial meeting over as soon as possible. The situation wasn't going to change even if she put him off until the end of the day, and she'd have it hanging over her, too.

'I'm free for the next three-quarters of an hour,' she began briskly, then realised that she'd automatically treated the room as her own domain, sitting at the desk as if it was her right. 'That is, I'll be free as soon as

I've had time to take my belongings out of your room…although where I'll be able to put them…' she finished under her breath, completely unable to think of anywhere in the department that she could set up as her own space. She'd been doing so much of the day-to-day running of the department for so long that there was very little in the room to remind her that it had actually been her former head of department's office.

'That's not important for the moment,' he said dismissively. 'We'll just have to share the office if there isn't anywhere else.'

Leah nearly choked at the impossibility of the idea. The room was far too small for a second desk to be shoehorned into the cramped space and they certainly couldn't share the existing one. What was he proposing? That she should sit on his lap?

'The important thing,' he continued while she fought to rid her brain of that seductive image, 'is that I need to be up to speed before I start work properly on Monday. Where we do it or whose name is on the door is immaterial.'

'So, what do you think of him?' Kelly demanded eagerly, her coat over her arm, at the end of her shift.

'Who?' Leah asked weakly, knowing it was a forlorn hope that the topic of conversation would be anything other than their new head of department.

'David ffrench, of course,' Kelly said impatiently, almost as though she doubted Leah's sanity. 'Remember? The man you've spent ages closeted with in that cosy little office, you lucky girl.'

'He's very different to Donald,' Leah said blandly, hoping that Kelly hadn't picked up on the fact that her heart had just performed a sudden jig at the mention of his name. It had been bad enough when he'd been standing in the office doorway and she'd been able to put the width of the desk between them, but sitting side by side with their elbows and knees in almost constant contact had quickly become torture. She'd never been this aware of *any* man, not even...

'Duh!' Kelly mocked, halting that particular train of thought before it could hit the buffers. 'Tell me something I *haven't* noticed! David ffrench is absolutely nothing like Donald, thank God. Tell me...while you were in here, what have you managed to find out about his private life? Is he married, engaged, living with a significant other or is he gloriously, wonderfully free to fall instantly in love with yours truly?'

'I haven't got a clue,' Leah replied honestly, but felt the tide of warmth seeping up her face with the silent admission that for the first time in a long time she'd actually found herself thinking exactly the same questions. 'All I can tell you is that he doesn't wear a ring—not that *that* is any indication of anything these days, especially for a surgeon.'

'Ah, so you were looking!' Kelly pounced.

'Not really, but I couldn't help noticing as we were working our way through the current case files.' And couldn't help noticing what nice hands he had either. They were all lean and long fingered and looked as if they had the sort of sinewy strength that any surgeon needed, combined with the delicacy of touch and fine control that was essential for their exacting specialty.

'So, do you think he'll be good for the department?' Kelly asked, suddenly reverting to a more serious frame of mind. 'Do you think you'll be able to work with him?'

'Time will tell,' Leah said noncommittally. 'He certainly seems to know his stuff.'

'And the fact that he's so easy on the eyes is a big help, too,' Kelly joked archly. 'Not that he seems very interested in playing the flirting game. I think nearly every female in the entire obs and gyn section perked up as he's gone by, but he didn't even seem to notice. Oh!' She gasped as a sudden thought struck her. 'You don't think he's…you know, batting for the other team?'

'You mean, homosexual?' Leah fought a grin, determined to at least appear to take the suggestion seriously. 'I suppose he could be. Once again, though, only time will tell.'

She was grinning openly as a scowling Kelly made her way out of the unit, muttering darkly that all the good-looking men were either married or gay, absolutely certain in her own mind that, married or not, David ffrench was a hundred per cent pure functioning male.

'Hey, big brother! How did it go today? Did you get a chance to look around your new domain?'

'Hi, Moggy! How are you doing?' David felt a wide smile spread over his face at the sound of his sister's voice at the other end of the phone, grateful for the chance to stop unpacking boxes. He lowered himself into his borrowed armchair and suddenly realised why it had been so eagerly donated when it nearly swallowed him whole. He might have to call for help just to escape from its smothering clutches. 'Is that new husband of yours treating you right?'

'Like a fragile piece of priceless china,' she grumbled, but he could hear the happiness underlying the complaint. It was so good to know that she'd finally found what she'd always wanted—a man who loved her every bit as much as she loved him—and if it left *him* feeling pea green with envy, that was his own problem. He'd thought he'd had it all once, and look where he was now.

'Perhaps that's because you're not only newly-weds but you're also pregnant with his baby,' he pointed out. 'And you know you wouldn't want it any other way.'

'True,' she conceded cheerfully and with a definite hint of smugness. 'Hey! No sidetracking! You didn't answer my question. What *did* you think of your new department? Are you glad I twisted your arm to apply for the post? Did you have a chance to meet Leah Dawson? What did you think of her? Don't you think she's just—?'

'Hey, Moggy! Give me a chance to answer the first half-dozen questions before you pile on the next dozen!' He chuckled, glad that she'd never grown out of that habit. He'd been teasing her about it ever since she'd learned to talk.

'Not so much of the Moggy!' she complained, as she always did. 'I'm not ten any more. So, start answering. Isn't Leah just great?'

For some reason that was the last question David felt like answering, and he couldn't think of a single logical reason why—at least, not one he cared to contemplate with his nosy little sister on the other end of the phone.

Hurriedly, he reverted to an earlier question.

'Yes, Moggy, I freely admit that I'm absolutely delighted that you brought the AR vacancy to my attention. It has the makings of an excellent department.'

'The makings? You mean, once you've done your new-broom bit and completely reorganised it?' she teased, but he knew there was more than a hint of the truth in her words. He did like to put his own stamp on the way his department was run, but he certainly didn't want to start off by alienating the existing staff.

He wondered just how well his sister knew Leah. Maggie and Jake hadn't needed the assistance of his new department to start her pregnancy, but she might have met his new colleague when they'd had to call for someone to take a look at a potential admission down in A and E. She might also have met her when she'd accompanied an emergency patient up to the department at some time.

Had she also noticed the chaotic disarray in his predecessor's office, with files on every available surface? It certainly wasn't the way he liked to run a department and he'd been amazed that Leah had apparently had no trouble putting her hand on everything he'd requested.

And there she was, back inside his head again, no matter how hard he tried to keep her out. He had far more important things to think about than a pair of serious grey eyes and a wealth of honey-blonde hair tied tightly back to reveal the delicate bone structure of her face.

He shook his head, glad that Maggie couldn't see him. What did it matter that his new colleague was tall and slender and filled with almost incandescent nervous energy? It certainly hadn't helped her to keep on top of a simple job like keeping the office straight. Come Monday, he dreaded discovering that her attention to other things, like the important details that should have been recorded in each of those case notes since her superior died, was equally slap-dash. In the short time she'd had free, he hadn't been able to do much more than get an idea of the scope of patients currently under investigation and treatment, and the general routine of the department on a daily and weekly basis.

'Would Jake be happy working in a disorganised department?' he challenged gently. 'I bet the first thing he did when he got his consultancy was go over every tiny detail in person.'

'And you'd win, you rat!' Maggie grumbled. 'Just promise me something—don't ruffle too many feathers on your first day. Take it gently until you've had a chance to get to know the people you'll be working with. They're a good tight-knit team.'

'Yes, Mother,' he said in a singsong voice. 'I'll play nicely with the other boys and girls.'

'Oh, you're impossible!' she spluttered. 'Sometimes I don't know why I bother.'

'Because I'm your lovable big brother?' he suggested, tongue in cheek.

'Exactly,' she said, heaving a theatrical put-upon sigh. 'But, seriously, David…'

'Uh-oh! When she uses those dreaded words…!' he teased. 'It's OK, Moggy. You can stop worrying about me, I'm a big boy now.'

'I know that, but I don't just want you to be successful, I want you to be happy, too,' she said plaintively.

The words hung in the air between them for several seconds.

David knew exactly what she meant. Since she'd found happiness with Jake, she wanted everyone to be equally happy, but he knew that wasn't possible for him. He'd had his chance and it had all gone horribly wrong.

'It wasn't your fault, David,' she said softly in his ear, and he shivered at the accuracy of the way she'd followed his thoughts. Was he really that transparent?

'That didn't make any difference to the pain,' he said gruffly, startled that he'd even admitted that much. In fact, it was probably the most he'd said to anyone about the loss that would haunt him for ever, and it would be the last. 'So, if you don't mind, little sister, I'll concentrate on my new job and making the department second to none. That'll make me happy.'

'But you can't take the department to bed for a cuddle,' she retorted stubbornly. 'David, you can't cut yourself off from people like that. If you don't want to talk to me, you could phone Mum and Dad. Calls to New Zealand may be expensive, but on your salary—'

'No way!' he exploded a second before he could put a guard on his tongue.

'What?' Maggie sounded startled. 'But, David, you've always been so close to them—they moved halfway round the world to be near you, for heaven's sake. Surely they'd be willing to listen if you wanted to talk?'

'Too damn close!' he muttered under his breath, then realised that he needed to make some sort of explanation.

'Mum and Dad—at least, *Mum*—is one of the reasons why I *left* New Zealand. I had to get away, Maggie. She was still trying to smother me, the way she did when I was a kid. I'm thirty-four, for heaven's sake! I don't need my mother to bandage my grazed knees and kiss them better!'

Maggie giggled. 'That's an image to conjure with!'

'Well, it's not so funny when you're on the receiving end of it,' he pointed out grimly.

'But, David—' she began persuasively, but he'd had enough.

'And you'd better watch your step,' he warned. 'If you're going to start nagging, I'll set Jake on you. I'll tell him that he needs to keep a closer eye on you.'

'Don't you dare!' she squealed in dismay. 'I can hardly breathe as it is. If somebody from Obs and Gyn told him I needed watching he'd never let me out of his sight.'

'That's because you and the baby mean that much to him,' he pointed out softly, the pain of memories tightening its grip around his throat and his heart. 'Enjoy every precious minute of it, Moggy. Sleep tight.'

'This isn't working,' Leah muttered as she stepped back from her little workbench in disgust.

Usually she could lose herself in the timeless art of repotting, trimming and training her precious bonsai trees, the cares of the day simply melting away as she put her concentration to each measured task. Tonight it just wasn't happening and it was all *his* fault.

'I might just as well be doing something useful, rather than risking spoiling one of you,' she muttered as she collected and cleaned her tools and put them away. 'And I know just the job.'

Decision made, it took mere moments before her hands were washed and she was reaching for her keys with a wry grimace. It would always seem wasteful to drive such a short distance, but it would be a very foolish woman who would wander about in the deep shadows between her flat and the hospital buildings in the dark.

Not long after that, she'd shut herself in the night-time seclusion of the untidy office and was rolling up her sleeves in preparation for the final stage in her reorganisation of Donald's filing system. The audit of all his files had been long overdue and a surprising number should already have been sent to the hospital archives. The remaining stacks were a far more manageable number for the available space in the filing cabinets.

She pulled open the first empty drawer and couldn't help chuckling when she remembered the horrified expression on David ffrench's face when he'd seen the chaos in the room. It had been sheer stubbornness mixed with her disappointment at losing out on the head of department job that had stopped her from explaining what was going on, and she felt a bit guilty about it now.

'Guilty enough to lose some sleep to finish the job, but as I've already checked the contents of each one of these and put them all into alphabetical order, at least this part should be a breeze,' she muttered as she prepared to slot each file into position. In a relatively short space of time she could have every last piece of paper filed neatly out of sight and she could push the last drawer shut with a warm feeling of achievement.

Suddenly she paused and threw a disparaging glare around the room.

'The trouble is, when there are none of Donald's piles of filing to distract the eye, it will be even more obvious just how shabby everything has become.'

The walls, in particular, could do with a fresh coat of paint—something rather more welcoming than

dingy Institution Beige. 'But fresher walls will make
the curtains look worse than ever,' she muttered in
defeat, until an image of the spare pair of curtains lurk-
ing back at her flat leapt into her head. She'd bought
them for her last flat and, while they didn't fit any of
the windows in her new one, they were still nearly
new.

'And if I can corner one of the maintenance men
some time tomorrow... Even if he can't do something
about it, perhaps I could get him to beg a can of paint
from the stores. Then I could come back again tomorrow evening...'

Course of action decided, she put the pile of files
back where she'd got them from, switched off the light
and locked the door behind her, a tiny smile betraying
the thought that she was actually looking forward to
David ffrench starting work on Monday. She could
hardly wait to see the expression on his face when he
saw the finished transformation.

'And it'll be every bit as good as any of the make-
overs he'd see on the television,' she vowed, a fresh
spring in her step in spite of the time.

David ffrench stepped back into the shadow of the
stairwell with a frown.

'What on earth is Leah Dawson doing here at this
time of night?' he muttered into the darkness, his eyes
following her swiftly moving figure as she made her
way to the lifts. She'd obviously been home since the
end of her shift because she'd changed from her neatly
tailored trousers into a pair of decidedly disreputable
jeans, jeans that revealed a figure every bit as neat and
slender as he'd imagined.

And that smile! It was the first one he'd seen that

didn't look as if it had been forced out of her by well-drilled manners, and it had instantly intrigued him.

What had she been doing in his office at this time of night…? Well, it would be his office when he took it over on Monday morning. His frown deepened as he considered the possibilities. She must be in her late twenties or early thirties, so far too old for juvenile pranks such as whoopee cushions, and he hoped that she was far too professional to do something as stupid as to mess about with patient files.

'As if I'd be able to tell,' he groaned softly, remembering the chaos littering every surface. 'As it is, it's going to take me a month of Sundays just to get things organised. How I'm going to be able to run the department at the same time…'

He couldn't imagine what the patients must think when they were shown into the room for the first time. It certainly wasn't confidence-inspiring, and the frustration was that he couldn't do anything about the situation until he officially started work.

'Unless…' he mused as he turned and made his way back down the stairs, then shook his head. The possibility of enlisting Leah in some overtime to sort through the mess had briefly flashed through his mind, but it wasn't a good idea.

'No,' he conceded. 'I've got enough to do in the next twenty-four hours with organising my living space. And I really don't need to get off on the wrong foot with Leah before we've even started to work together.'

As he left, he smiled absently at the security guard who'd earlier verified his identity before admitting him to the building, then lengthened his stride as he set off towards the nearby block of flats, wondering why the woman seemed to have taken up permanent residence inside his head when he'd only met her this morning.

'The last thing I need is getting tangled up with some woman,' he said aloud, startling an elderly gentleman taking his equally elderly dog out for its late-night constitutional. 'Been there, done that,' he muttered more quietly. 'I've got the scars to prove it.'

CHAPTER TWO

'THAT looks better!' Leah exclaimed aloud as she clambered down from her perch on the window-sill and stepped back to admire her handiwork.

In the distance, she heard the chimes of the church clock striking two, a reassuring sound that couldn't be heard at all when the department was busy during the day, but now only served to remind her of just how late it was.

'If I'm going to be awake enough to work a full shift, I'd better get home to bed,' she muttered. 'I wouldn't want to oversleep and miss out on seeing his reaction.'

She'd already deposited the decorating equipment in a nearby storage cupboard, as arranged with the helpful maintenance man. Now that she'd hung the curtains, she was going to leave the window open for the rest of the night to help to dispel the last of the paint fumes.

'Now *I'm* the messiest thing in the room,' she said with a grimace for her paint-splattered clothing, but the results were certainly well worthwhile.

In spite of her need to get home, get cleaned up and get some sleep, she couldn't help pausing by the door for a little gloat at all she'd achieved.

She'd barely had time to rejoice over the improvement—the calm, professional appearance of the 'business' end of the room, with not a stray piece of paper to be seen, compared to the softer, more welcoming area where prospective parents would be invited to sit—when her pager shrilled its imperative summons, startling her out of her wits.

'I hope it's a misdialled code,' she muttered even as she was reaching for the receiver to answer the call.

'Leah? How long will it take you to get here?' demanded the familiar voice of one of the midwives.

'Is there a problem?' Leah made a sound of disgust. 'Ignore the stupid question, Sally. Blame it on the time of night and change it to "What's the problem?"'

'Major, *major* problem,' she said grimly. 'An IVF patient in advanced labour, multiple birth, malpresentation.'

Already Leah's head was reeling with the staccato presentation of facts. One part of her brain was sifting through 'their' patients, but she couldn't think of any of the sets of twins who were anywhere near due yet.

'Which one? Is she miscarrying?' Unfortunately, there was a high rate of loss and all its attendant heartaches in their vulnerable group of patients.

'Not one of ours,' Sally reassured her succinctly. 'She's in a bad way. How soon can you get here? I think the only way we're going to save any of them is an emergency Caesarean, pronto, and Chas is already fully occupied.'

For just a fleeting second she wondered if she was about to bite off more than she could chew. This would be her first really complicated case since Donald had died, and although he hadn't delivered a baby for several years, there had been a certain sense of security in knowing that such an experienced man had been nearby.

'How long will it take you to get her into Theatre?' She glanced across at the clock on the wall above the filing cabinets to confirm the time while she contemplated her course of action. 'I'll go straight there and start to scrub.'

'Ten minutes, tops. I've already warned Theatre to get ready,' Sally informed her, then added, 'Leah, make it as fast as you can, please. I've got a really bad feeling about this one.'

The butterflies in Leah's stomach became helicopters with those parting words. Sally was an experienced midwife not prone to panicking at the slightest hitch. If she was worried, then there was something to worry about and even though she could have taken the case on herself, Leah knew what she had to do. With mother and babies' lives at stake, this was no time for egos or hospital politics.

'Hello, Switchboard, I need to contact one of the consultants urgently, and I don't have his home number,' she announced briskly, her fingers crossed that the computer had already been updated ready for David ffrench's commencement today at a more civilised time. It only briefly crossed her mind that his insurance cover might not start until he was officially on duty. 'It's David ffrench…two f's. He's the new appointment to Obs and Gyn.'

It took several more precious minutes to persuade the person on the other end that if *they* made the connection to the outside line, they wouldn't actually be breaking his right to confidentiality.

'H'lo?' said a husky voice right in her ear, and every nerve quivered with the knowledge that she'd just woken him up, that he was probably lying in his bed—totally naked?—with his dark hair all rumpled and…

'Mr ffrench?' she squeaked, and had to clear her throat before she could continue, gabbling in her em-

barrassment at her unruly imagination. 'I'm sorry to
disturb you when you haven't officially begun working
here, but could you possibly come over to the hospital?
There's an emergency Caesarean…multiple birth…
And I think I'm going to need you. Oh, this is Leah
Dawson.'

'Foetal distress?' he demanded, already obviously
firing on all cylinders, much to Leah's envy. She still
hated being woken in the middle of the night, even
after all these years in the profession. 'How many
weeks gestation and how long has the mother been in
labour?'

'I don't know much more than I've told you,' she
admitted. 'But it was Sally Ling, one of the most experienced midwives in the department, who called me,
and she knows what she's talking about. Chas—
Charles Westmoreland—isn't available because he's
already dealing with a problem delivery,' she added,
anticipating his next question.

'I can be there in ten minutes. Get her into Theatre,'
he said tersely, and before she could utter a word of
thanks, he'd broken the connection.

Leah could have wasted energy feeling snubbed by
his abruptness, but all she was conscious of was relief
that he was on his way. Now it was time to get moving.

'Have you got any more details for me?' she demanded over her shoulder as she began the scrubbing
ritual, the cotton of the theatre greens feeling very thin
and insubstantial after her jeans.

Sally's head appeared round the corner, her dark
curls already trying to escape from the disposable cap.

'Mum tried to tell me that she's thirty-eight, but I'd
say she's much closer to sixty.'

'What?' Leah gaped at her, hands suspended in mid-scrub. 'You're joking! She probably just looks a bit…shattered after carrying a double load around for so many months.'

'You could be right,' Sally said dubiously. 'See what you think when you see her. Ashraf's not too happy about any of it. We've got absolutely no previous notes and she's being extremely cagey about where she had her treatment, and he's in charge of her anaesthesia.'

'Not another one!' exclaimed David as he joined Leah at the sink. He'd obviously heard enough of the conversation as he'd come in to pick up on what was happening. 'We had one like this at my last post. Apparently she'd had extensive cosmetic surgery so that she could use her niece's passport for identification as she was well beyond the age limits for properly regulated IVF. We never did find out where she'd been treated and we nearly lost her to eclampsia.'

'Oh, boy, am I glad I invited you to this little party,' Leah groaned. 'By the way, should I make the introductions? David ffrench, new head of our little domain, meet Sally Ling, midwife *extraordinaire*.'

'I take it this is what's called being thrown in at the deep end,' David commented as he took his turn at having the ties fastened at the back of his gown, then held his hands out for gloves.

'We wouldn't like you to think you were going to be bored here, so we thought we'd lay on a bit of entertainment,' Sally quipped, taking another look into the room behind her. 'I think Ashraf's nearly ready for you to begin, but he doesn't look happy.'

'Too right, Ashraf's not happy!' exclaimed the man in question, his dark eyes firmly fixed on the array of monitors grouped at his end of the table. 'Some things are just not right.'

'Is there a problem with her anaesthesia?' Leah heard the sharp edge of concern in David's voice.

'You mean, apart from the fact that her blood pressure's too high and her lungs aren't the best?' he said wryly. 'No, what I meant was that I reckon we can add at least twenty years to the age the patient's given us, and a woman in her fifties or sixties should be looking forward to grandchildren, the way nature intended. There are sound physiological reasons why there should be age limits for IVF. *And* it's a multiple birth!' he finished, the words almost completely incomprehensible as his accent became stronger and stronger in his passion.

'You'll get no argument from me,' David said grimly as he painted the grossly swollen abdomen preparatory to the incision. 'And to turn up obviously *intending* to leave us completely in the dark about the details of her pregnancy…!'

He didn't bother finishing the sentence, but Leah knew he didn't need to when everyone in the room knew just how much that omission could affect the outcome of what they were doing.

'Is everybody ready?' he asked, and Leah threw one last look around the assembled staff. Apart from those grouped around the operating table, there were two teams waiting in the background with the high-tech Perspex incubators for the other two tiny individuals who would hopefully be joining them in the room soon. What they were going to do if both babies needed high-dependency nursing was another problem entirely. There were never enough beds or specially trained staff to cope, and they would need to do some

serious juggling with the babies already in the unit to
cope with just one seriously sick preemie. A second
one would probably have to face a life-threatening
dash to whichever NICU had the nearest free HDU
bed. She'd probably have to spend several hours on
the phone begging and pleading...

But that was in the future. First they had to deliver
the babies.

'Ready,' she confirmed as she turned back to the
table. Those striking eyes were waiting for her, somehow all the more potent for the fact that they were all
she could see of him above his disposable mask. For
just a second it almost felt as if the two of them had
made some sort of silent connection but then he had
his hand out ready to receive the scalpel, and when he
immediately applied it to their patient's skin in an
expert arc she knew she must have been mistaken.

It was lovely to watch him work, she thought, admiring the efficient way he'd exposed the uterus.
Without a word needing to be spoken, she was ready
to zap the inevitable bleeders then stood poised with
suction as he carefully chose the site for the second
incision. The last thing they needed was to injure one
of the babies with an injudicious cut.

Amniotic fluid gushed out of the widening aperture
and he had to pause for a moment before he could
insert two fingers into the gap as a guide, positioning
them between the wall of the uterus and the babies it
contained to enable him to continue cutting.

'It's all arms and legs in here,' he muttered as he
inserted one long-fingered hand through the incision.
'Ah! Gotcha! Leah?' he nodded towards the exposed
belly above the incision.

She placed one hand on the strangely brown flesh

and waited for his signal, but he hardly needed her assistance, the baby's head emerging cradled in his palm and the rest of the spindly body following in a rapid slither.

'It's a girl!' Leah announced as the cord was cut and she immediately turned to place the wriggling infant into the waiting warmed blanket held out by Sally just as she let out her first wail.

'One down, one to go,' David said as he inserted his hand again, this time emerging with a tiny foot and going back to find the other one of the pair. 'Come on, sunshine,' he said encouragingly. 'There's a lot of people out here waiting to meet you.'

Leah smiled behind her mask, once more poised for the nod that would come if he needed help to get the baby's head out into the world.

'It's another girl,' she said, the sex of the baby all too obvious in such an undignified position, then it was time to cut the cord and hand her little charge over to the second waiting team.

She turned back, expecting to find David dealing with the clean removal of two placentas, but found him scowling darkly.

'I don't believe it!' he exclaimed. 'There's a third one in here!'

'What!' Leah gasped, unable to believe her ears.

For a second nobody moved, then they all spoke at once.

'You're joking!'

'We'll need another team with an incubator. Hurry.'

'Her blood pressure's dropping.'

It was the final voice that silenced them all, and while Leah knew that there was frantic activity behind her as extra help was summoned from the NICU, she was focusing solely on David.

If she hadn't been so close to him for the last half-hour she probably wouldn't have noticed the new urgency in his movements, but, as it was, she could almost feel the tension emanating from him.

'Come on, come on!' she heard him mutter under his breath, almost growling with frustration.

Perhaps his hands were too large for the job, even though they were relatively slender for a man. Perhaps her smaller ones would help—anything to bring the unexpected third baby out successfully.

'Do you want me to—?'

'Got it!' he exclaimed, interrupting her offer before it had been made. 'It was a transverse lie and the poor little thing had been squashed by its sisters trying to get out.'

Even as he was speaking he was lifting the tiny scrap out of its mother's body, and Leah's heart clenched when she saw the state the infant was in.

'He's terribly floppy!' she exclaimed, already reaching out to take the precious burden. 'Is he breathing?'

She didn't really want to pass the tiny being over, all her protective instincts demanding she take care of it herself, but with Ashraf's renewed warning that they needed to finish the operation as soon as possible, all she could do was relinquish her into Sally's waiting hands, knowing that her colleague would do everything she could.

In the meantime, there were now three placentas to remove and check for completeness before the incisions in both uterus and skin could be closed—and all with the clock ticking ominously.

'Damn! Where is all that blood coming from?'

David swore suddenly. 'Leah, suction! I can't see what's going on…'

'Hurry up, guys,' Ashraf warned. 'We're going to lose her.'

'Not without a fight,' David countered fiercely. 'Get some more fluids into her as fast as you can,' he directed as he peered into the gaping wound. 'Damn it, the uterus is paper thin. It's almost shredding as we look at it.'

'You'll have to do a hysterectomy,' Leah said, hoping she sounded calmer than she felt. 'With blood loss this rapid there isn't time for any sort of repair, not if she's going to be around for those babies.'

David met her eyes for the briefest moment and she knew that they'd both come to that same decision.

She'd thought she'd seen him working quickly before, but it was nothing to the speed at which he excised the life-threatening tissue in a room filled with the din of shrilling monitors warning of imminent disaster.

'She's going to crash!' Ashraf called, and out of the corner of her eye Leah could see his hands flying from one control to another as he tried his best to support their failing patient.

'Thirty seconds, Ashraf!' David growled, without pausing for a single one of them in his determination to cheat death. 'Just keep her going for another thirty seconds.'

'I'll do my best, but I can't promise you've got even that long,' the anaesthetist warned as the monitor told them that their patient's heart was beating almost out of control in an attempt to circulate the remaining blood, but David didn't even falter.

Leah was aware of a strange feeling that was almost

exhilaration as she assisted in one of the most frantic operations she'd ever witnessed. For the first time ever in an operation, the lead surgeon didn't even need to say what he wanted. Somehow she just knew and was there ready with the next clamp or the diathermy to seal off another bleeding blood vessel.

'Bowl,' David said, even as Leah was holding it out to him. He finally glanced towards Ashraf. 'How is she doing?'

'Holding her own—just,' he said cautiously, and checked all his monitors again. 'We're actually managing to get some volume into her, now that she's not leaking like a sieve. Her heart rate is coming down and her blood pressure's coming up.'

'In that case, Leah, would you like to close?' He raised one dark eyebrow but she was more interested in the expression of relief she detected in those beautiful eyes.

'Oh, yes. Of course,' she floundered, feeling like a fool for standing gazing at him like that. What on earth was going on? She'd never behaved like this before. Imagine—standing in the operating theatre in the middle of a procedure and thinking that the new consultant had beautiful eyes!

Whatever next? she demanded silently as she did a final check to make sure that nothing was bleeding any more, then carefully sutured the abdominal musculature layer by layer.

'Nice neat job,' David murmured at her elbow, but she'd known that he was watching, every nerve seeming to recognise his proximity even though she couldn't see him.

'Thank you, sir,' she said with a mock curtsey, then stepped back to allow others to take over the application of protective dressings before their patient was taken through to Recovery.

'And may I return the compliment, in spades,' she continued, when they'd made their way out of Theatre to divest themselves of their liberally splattered clothing. Sudden nervousness at the thought that he was about to see her in nothing more than her underwear made her chatter. 'I've never seen anyone work that fast or that accurately, and I'll be eternally grateful that you agreed to come in tonight. I know I could have delivered the babies, but I doubt whether I'd have been able to save the mother when it all went pear-shaped so quickly.'

Suddenly confronted by the tanned width of his naked chest, her tongue stopped working, her jaw all but hanging open. Had she thought he was too thin? She could obviously blame his tailor because there was nothing wrong with the body she was seeing in front of her...close enough to touch if she just reached out...

'You'll be surprised what you can manage to do when there aren't any other options,' he said quietly, jerking her out of that dangerous line of thought, then a glint of mischief lit his eyes. 'And I like the sound of *eternally grateful*. Does that translate into fetching cups of coffee?'

'In your dreams!' she retorted, grateful that he hadn't noticed the way she was eyeing him and surprised that he felt at ease enough to tease. The rather solemn man she'd met the other day hadn't looked as if he had a single joke in him.

'But you'd join me in one?'

She glanced up at the clock and pulled a face.

'I may as well,' she agreed. 'It certainly isn't worth

going back to bed now, and I'm going to need plenty of it, strong and sweet, if I'm going to stay awake today.'

'Well, shall we agree that the first one out of the shower pours the coffee?' he suggested. 'How do you like yours, exactly?'

'You're making the assumption that you'll finish first,' she pointed out sweetly. 'I like mine strong but white with just a dash of sugar—how do you take yours?'

'White. Without,' he said, then grinned. 'I'll see you in a few minutes, then. Your coffee should have cooled enough to drink by the time you get there,' he added in what was clearly a challenge.

David tensed when he heard the door open behind him, wondering how he could possibly know that it was Leah who had just entered.

He was surprised to see that there was a slight tremor to the hand that was pouring the coffee when it had been perfectly steady in the life-and-death situation just a few minutes ago in Theatre.

'Drat!' he heard her say, and knew that it was in response to the fact that he'd beaten her.

He quickly stretched a triumphant smile over his face and turned to face her with a coffee in each hand, and nearly dropped both of them.

He certainly wouldn't have expected her hair to be that long, and to see it hanging all the way to the middle of her back, still dripping with water, sent his imagination into overdrive…until he hastily put the brakes on it. He was still having difficulty trying to forget the sight of her elegant curves clothed in nothing more than creamy lace underwear as she'd stripped off after surgery.

Now was not the time for mental images of Leah in the shower, slick, wet hair flowing over her naked body, not while she was standing in front of him with her hand held out for the coffee he was clutching like a lifeline.

'All right, I concede,' she said. 'But under duress. If I cut my hair as short as yours I'd be able to—'

'Don't!' he exclaimed in horror at the idea. It was only when he saw the surprise on her face that he realised he'd spoken aloud and was abashed to feel the slow crawl of heat up his face. Was he blushing like a gauche teenager, for heaven's sake? What was this woman doing to him? 'I mean, it must have taken you years to grow it that long. It would be such a shame to just…' He was making it worse, he realised when he saw her fighting a grin.

'It would grow again,' she said with a shrug, apparently totally unconcerned by the prospect of destroying what used to be called a woman's crowning glory. 'I'd even thought of getting people to sponsor me to have my head shaved, to raise money for charity.'

'*Shaved!*' He was definitely horrified. 'Well, would you take offers *not* to cut it?' he countered, while a tiny voice inside his head tried hard to remind him that this woman was little more than a stranger and there was absolutely no reason why she should take any notice of his wishes.

'Now, that's another possibility,' she said as she put her cup down and casually twisted the length of her hair into a thick rope and wound it neatly against the back of her head, securing it with a giant clip. 'But sometimes I think it's not worth the bother and all the time it takes. After all, with a shaven head, I would easily have beaten you to the coffee.'

She took a careful sip to test the temperature then a larger mouthful when she found it bearable. He nearly groaned aloud when she closed her eyes and moaned in ecstasy.

'Why does the first cup of the day taste so good?' she demanded.

He didn't reply. The memory of waking up to other activities, and the realisation of just how long ago that had been, reminded him with a jolt of all the reasons why he shouldn't be indulging in this sparring with her. It wasn't right, not when he had absolutely no intention of following through. His days on the relationship merry-go-round were over, and he was glad of it. He wouldn't willingly go through that pain again for anything.

'I stuck my head round the door to check up on the babies,' he announced, needing to get his thoughts onto more professional matters. As that was the only sort of relationship the two of them could have, he might just as well set the boundaries right from the start. 'Baby three—the little boy who got squashed— wasn't doing very well, but his big sisters were doing amazingly well, in spite of their size and prematurity.'

'And Mum?'

'Still in Recovery. Ashraf's hovering over her. All her vital signs seem to be slowly coming good but she hasn't really shaken off the anaesthetic yet.' He frowned briefly. 'She's certainly not compos mentis enough to be told what happened on the table.'

'Well, that's certainly going to be an interesting set

of notes to write up. Perhaps you could make a presentation of the case at the monthly meeting.'

'A presentation?' He was startled by the suggestion.
At his last post he'd barely had time to breathe, let
alone prepare presentations, then he realised how logical the suggestion was when she continued.

'Not only would it serve as a cautionary tale for
those who weren't involved today, but it would also
scotch the rumours that are bound to grow with every
telling.'

'Ah, yes. The hospital grapevine,' he said ruefully.
'That's one aspect of our job that's the same wherever
we go—a hairline crack becomes multiple fractures and
a Caesarean delivery and hysterectomy becomes—'

'A life-saving procedure performed superbly to give
mother and all three babies the best chance possible,'
she interrupted, and for the first time in a long time,
in spite of his embarrassment, he allowed himself a
brief moment to bask in the warmth of her praise.

'Which I couldn't have attempted without a damn
good team to back me up,' he added, giving them their
due, too. 'Ashraf's definitely one of the best anaesthe-
tists I've worked with. That woman was emptying out
so fast…' He shook his head at the scary memory. 'I
honestly don't know how he kept her going long
enough for me to tie everything off. And as for you…'

It was her turn to blush, but he wasn't giving her
empty words—he wouldn't waste his time on anything
but the truth.

'I admit that I was quite surprised to hear that you
were one of the applicants for the AR head of department. I couldn't believe that someone so young could
possibly have the necessary skills.' He bowed briefly

towards her. 'Suffice it to say that since I've witnessed your skill and intuition, albeit assisting this time rather than leading, I'm no longer surprised. You knew exactly what I was going to do and how to make it easy for me—proof, in spite of your own doubts, that you would have been equally able to do the job.'

She was obviously trying to bury her embarrassment in her coffee-cup but he could tell that she was pleased with his recognition of her skills. He had a brief image of the chaos that awaited him in his office and suppressed a shudder that it had been allowed to get into such a state. Was it just that organisation was not one of her skills? He supposed he had to make allowances for the fact that she'd been trying to run the department short-handed, but just in case her weakness *was* paperwork, he was going to offer to write up this morning's case notes himself.

'Are you sure?' she said doubtfully. 'Donald hated doing them—said he'd rather have his teeth pulled.'

'I'm sure,' he said with an even deeper sense of foreboding. Had he been unlucky enough to take over a department that hadn't had anyone willing to take on the essentials? 'I've brought everything with me and I shall have another cup or three of coffee while I get it done.'

'In that case, I'm going to check up on Mum then sneak in for a peep at the babies. I wonder if anyone's been able to contact their father yet.'

'I'll leave you to check up on that and I'll see you in my office at, say, eight?' he suggested.

For just a moment there was a strange expression on her face but it was gone too quickly for him to decipher it. Was it chagrin that it was now *his* office rather than hers, or was it the fact that she was handing it over in such a disastrous state? Well, either way, there was nothing she could do about it now. The job was his, and, providing there wasn't a run of emergencies like this morning's, it really shouldn't take him long to get everything organised, even if he had to ask Personnel for the temporary loan of some sort of specialist filing clerk.

In the meantime, he had a complicated surgery to document, right down to the last suture and cc of drugs. At least *that* ought to push Leah out of his mind until he saw her again at eight.

CHAPTER THREE

'HELLO... Ah, g-good morning, sir,' Leah ended up stammering, suddenly unaccountably uncertain as to what she should call her new boss.

Working together in Theatre in such fraught conditions had definitely given her a feeling of connection with him, but perhaps he preferred a little more formality from the more junior members of his...

'Sir?' he queried with a blink, then ostentatiously looked over his shoulder as if looking for someone else she might be addressing.

Leah couldn't help the brief giggle that escaped her. It was probably the result of the nerves that had built up while she was trying not to look as if she was hovering around in the corridor, waiting for him to arrive. She'd even unlocked the door in preparation for his arrival, in case he hadn't been given his own set of keys yet.

Then he'd swept open the door at the other end of the corridor and begun striding towards her, all long lean legs and broad shoulders, and all her rational thought processes had ceased.

'That's better,' he said with an answering smile as he reached for the door handle. 'Obviously, there has to be a degree of formality when there are patients present, but at all other times you're free to call me... God! What on earth happened here?'

He took a step back to look at the name-plate on the door, as though doubting that he'd come to the right room, but even *that* had been changed after she'd chased Maintenance to install his name in place of Donald's—just one of the last-minute things she'd done while he'd been occupied writing up the post-op notes.

His reaction was everything she could have hoped for, but it was his slip of the tongue that actually made her laugh aloud. It was a struggle to speak for several seconds.

'So, let me get this right,' she said, smiling in the face of his frown of puzzlement. 'You don't want formality but I'm free to call you… *God*?' she teased.

He was walking warily towards the miraculously clear desk.

'You know I didn't mean that,' he objected distractedly as he turned in a circle. 'When did all this happen and who did it?' he demanded, then she saw panic take over from approval. 'What happened to all the files, Leah? Where are they? They haven't been taken away, have they?'

'They're all here,' she soothed, taking the bunch of keys out of her pocket and selecting the correct one to open the first filing cabinet. 'And all in their proper alphabetical order, too.'

'But…I only saw this room on Friday…'

'And you've been having nightmares about it ever since,' Leah finished for him. 'The walls were dingy, the curtains were limp, drab and sun-bleached and there was paperwork on every horizontal surface.'

'Exactly!' he agreed. 'So…who, what, when, why and how? Obviously when I saw it before you must have known that the room was due for a visit from Maintenance for some overdue redecoration.'

'Not exactly.' She knew it was time to come clean.

His surprise had been everything she'd hoped for, but she wanted him to know the real reason for the chaos he'd stumbled into on his first visit. The last thing she wanted was for her new boss to think that had been the way she'd been happy to run the department. That impression might linger and could affect what he wrote about her when she needed a reference when another AR department headship came up.

She refused to let herself ponder the fact that the idea of leaving St Luke's had suddenly become much less attractive than it had been when she'd been told about David's appointment. She needed to concentrate on making her explanation.

'Maintenance were here this morning to install your name-plate and they also supplied the paint and brushes over the weekend.'

'And?' he prompted. 'Am I to take it that *you* provided the labour? When on earth did you find the time with all the hours you've been putting in on keeping the department running?'

'Well, it only took a couple of hours one evening to give everything a once-over.' And another couple for a second coat when the dinginess refused to disappear the first time, she added silently, but he didn't need to know that. Anyway, she wasn't into blowing her own trumpet. 'And the curtains were a spare set I had at home. They've hardly been used but they don't fit any of the windows in my new flat.'

'OK, so that's how the décor changed, but what about all the piles of paperwork? You certainly couldn't have sorted through all that and filed it away in a couple of hours one evening.'

'Actually, that's almost exactly how long it took,' she said giving him a smug smile, forgiving herself again for exaggerating a bit. After all, a doctor was well used to late nights, whether it was to deliver triplets or to sort out patient case notes. 'I'd already completed an audit of all the files, so some of the piles you saw on Friday were ready for collection to be archived. As for the rest, the only reason why I hadn't returned them to the filing cabinets was because that would have made them too heavy to move when I decorated.'

'And you achieved the whole thing in a weekend!' he marveled, and she didn't correct him with details of the many weeks it had taken to do the audit in the first place. She'd been horrified to find that Donald had probably avoided auditing his files ever since he'd come to the department, and the overfilled cabinets were the reason why the current patients' files had permanently littered the room, albeit in relatively tidy piles.

She'd actually believed that she'd been doing the tedious job for her own benefit, hoping that *she'd* get the appointment, but as it turned out…

'Well, I can't tell you how grateful I am that you went to all this trouble.' He spread his arms to indicate the whole pristine room. 'Not only will it be nicer—and more efficient—to work in, but it will look far more welcoming to the patients. And…' He drew the word out, suddenly pacing across the room and back again with a determined expression on his face.

'Yes! I thought so,' he announced. 'Now that you've removed all those boxes and piles, you've made enough room—if my desk is moved just a little further across—to juggle another desk in here, so you won't have to be served with an eviction order after all.'

That was the *last* thing she'd expected him to say,

and while her heart had suddenly taken up a faster beat
at the thought of sharing this room with him on a daily
basis, her reason was telling her that he would probably be such a distraction that she'd never get any
work done. She'd have to do some careful juggling of
her own to make sure that she only came in here when
he was otherwise occupied.

'I'll contact Maintenance and find out how to get
hold of another desk,' she said, bowing to the inevitable. It wasn't as if she'd been able to think of anywhere else to park herself. As one of the newer dis-
ciplines, the AR department had been forced to carve
itself a niche at one end of the obs and gyn department,
and space was at a premium.

'Great!' he said, clearly satisfied with finding a solution to her problem so swiftly. Equally obviously, he
was totally undisturbed by the fact they would end up
all but joined at the hip. 'Now, show me again how to
get this beast to let me know what's in the diary.' He
gestured towards the computer.

'Make sure it's switched on first,' she began with a
straight face. 'And then—'

'Smart alec!' he scowled. 'You do it this time. Come
here and sit down at the desk.'

Leah sat in what had so recently been *her* chair to
switch the computer on, and as David leaned over her
shoulder to watch what she was doing, she rued her
unruly tongue. It was actually very simple to access
the program and she could easily have explained without having him get so close.

Unfortunately, the fact that she was surrounded by
a mixture of soap, shampoo and something that could
only be David's skin, must have short-circuited a few

brain cells because it took her two unnecessary attempts to bring up that day's diary.

'So, according to this, starting at nine we have back-to-back appointments with new patients referred by their GPs. Is that usual?'

'What? That they're referred or that they're back-to-back?' Had his meaning been clear and it was his proximity that was muddling her?

'Both, I suppose.' He straightened up from his position leaning over her shoulder and she silently sighed in relief, but then he perched one hip on the corner of the desk, so she was no better off, her eyes drawn to the firm muscles in the thigh just inches from her hand. 'And why are they all new patients?'

Leah forced herself to look away, concentrating on the list of names on the screen while she gathered her thoughts.

'Donald set it up so he saw the new ones all on the same day, but there's no reason why you can't change the system if you want to. It was just *his* preference.' She chanced a glance in his direction and, when she found his intent gaze fixed unwaveringly on her, hurriedly looked away again. 'As for the referrals, as you know, this AR department is a centre of excellence and that means all the GPs within our catchment area are free to refer. That also includes obs and gyn departments in other hospitals that don't have a specialist AR department like ours.'

'And how does the lab cope with such a sudden influx? Do you have to give them special warning?'

'Yes and no,' Leah said with a smile. 'As referrals, most of the patients have already undergone the most basic tests through their GPs, so we only have to do the more specialised stuff. All our samples are sent direct to Stanley, who wouldn't hear of anyone else in the labs handling them.' She smiled as she digressed. 'Do you know, he actually resents having to take his annual leave because someone else has to do them while he's away? He says it takes him weeks to get everything running smoothly again.'

'A bit obsessive, is he?'

'No, just very grateful for the twins the department helped him and his wife to have after years of disappointment,' she explained with a reminiscent smile for the photos that Stanley always carried with him. 'He actually took himself off to learn the specific techniques he'd need for our work.'

'Well, when we've finished with this morning's list, you'll have to take me down and introduce me. He's someone I need to stay on the right side of, by the sound of it,' he said with a brief chuckle.

It was a sound that could even warm her deep inside where she'd thought the ice of disappointment would live for ever. The sensation that things were changing was more than a little frightening.

She didn't want anything to change. She'd already made the decision on the direction her life was going to take because it couldn't be any other way. She had no option.

Her profession. That was what mattered. That was all that mattered in her life now.

'The afternoon is a little more fluid,' she continued, hurriedly dragging her thoughts back to the screen in front of her. 'What you'll be doing then depends on the results of the blood tests and the ultrasounds— whether there'll be any mums ready to have their eggs harvested. There may be any number from none to eleven today.'

'And Stanley could cope if it was eleven?' David sounded very doubtful. That sort of lab work was painstaking and time-consuming, to say nothing of the strain on the eyes and the back from gazing down a microscope.

'If it meant a childless couple had their chance of parenthood, yes, he would, even if he had to work all night,' Leah confirmed quietly. 'Sometimes none of us get much sleep, especially when we have a group of mums whose cycles synchronise the way these seem to have done.'

She was prevented from saying any more by the imperious summons of the telephone. Without thinking, she reached out to pick it up, only to have David's long fingers land on top of hers.

'Oops! Sorry!' She jerked her tingling hand back. 'Force of habit. Let me—' She tried to relinquish her seat to him.

'It's all right. Stay put,' he said with one hand now on her shoulder as he lifted the receiver.

'Obstetrics and Gynaecology,' he announced, and then listened to the speaker on the other end, but Leah wasn't interested in eavesdropping on his conversation. She was far more interested in the discovery that he had inordinately long eyelashes, their existence disguised by the fact that the tip of each one had been lightened to gold by the New Zealand sun.

'Yes, this is David ffrench speaking. How can I help you?' he was saying, just as there was the sound of impatient knocking at the door.

He glanced across, then stepped away from Leah, finally releasing her from her position in the chair.

In response to his silently mouthed request, she set off towards the door, but before she could get there it was flung open and a florid-faced man stormed into the room.

'Are you Dr Dawson?' he demanded abruptly.

'I am,' she confirmed, quite taken aback. 'And you are?'

'*I* am one of the hospital's senior administrators,' he announced grandly, then totally ignored her, turning his fulminating gaze on the man just putting down the telephone. 'And you, I suppose, are Dr ffrench.'

'*Mr* ffrench,' Leah corrected swiftly.

He ignored her, directing his words solely to her new head of department.

'Well, I hope your slapdash behaviour today isn't an indication of how you intend to run this department—or do good manners not mean anything to you once you become a consultant?'

'I *beg* your pardon!' David said with enough ice in his voice to reverse a century of global warming.

'Well, I should think so, too,' the man continued, completely missing his meaning. 'Half an hour ago you were supposed to attend a brief reception to welcome you to St Luke's…'

'So your secretary has just informed me,' he interrupted frostily with a gesture towards the phone, '*and* without a single word of apology.'

Leah could remember the woman's self-righteous voice all too well. She'd actually tried to make it sound as if it was *Leah's* fault that she hadn't been informed earlier that the head of department position had gone to someone else.

'Don't talk rubbish, man,' scoffed the administrator. 'The press were all there—with photographers—and you wasted everybody's time and money! The least you could have done is informed us that you couldn't be bothered to attend, although why you would refuse, I can't—'

'Excuse me!' Leah interrupted sharply, stepping right in front of the obnoxious little man. For just a second she was inordinately glad that her smart heels meant that he had to crane his jowly head back to look up at her. Her blood was boiling that a jumped-up, overweight pencil-pusher should be so rude to such a skilful doctor. Without David's willingness to help this morning, regardless of the possibility of a court case if his insurance wasn't yet in force, there would be three babies without a mother.

'Didn't you listen to what Mr ffrench said?' she demanded heatedly. 'He *couldn't* go to your little party because your secretary *forgot* to send him his invitation, exactly the same as she *forgot* to inform me that I was going to be getting a new head of department until five minutes before he arrived.'

Out of the corner of her eye she saw David's hand go up to cover his mouth, but whether it was to prevent himself speaking or to warn her not to say any more she didn't know. It didn't make any difference anyway. There were things she needed to get off her chest.

'You claim you're worried about the waste of money?' she continued while the administrator was still gaping at her. 'Well, I've got a *wonderful* money-saving suggestion for you. I don't know how much you pay your secretary, but if you sack her, you'll save the hospital thousands because she's got the memory span of a geriatric goldfish and she's totally useless at her job.'

Even while the obnoxious man was gobbling speechlessly, David took over, grasping him by the elbow and directing him firmly out of the door.

'Thank you for your visit, but my colleague and I have a busy department to run and our first patients will be arriving any minute,' he announced gruffly, and closed the door in the administrator's purple face.

Leah was shaking with a combination of shock that she'd actually said all those things and nervousness at David's reaction. And she'd so wanted to get off on the right foot with him, especially as they were going to be working together so closely.

Then he turned round and she realised that his gruffness hadn't been displeasure at her lack of courtesy towards the administrator—no matter how pompous— but a cover for the urge to laugh.

'A geriatric goldfish?'

There was nothing stopping him now, and the rich sound filling the room sent a sudden wave of warmth through her as she joined in helplessly.

They were both wiping tears of mirth from their eyes when they finally managed to catch their breath.

'Oh, dear. How often am I likely to meet up with that delightful gentleman?' David said with a grimace.

'Never again, if you're lucky. I've certainly never met him before, so either he's new to the post and desperate to make his mark, or—as I was only caretaking your position—he never thought me worthy of a visit.'

'Well, going on first impressions, I wouldn't—'

'Oh, *please*, don't go on first impressions!' she exclaimed. 'I've explained why everything was in such a mess on Friday.'

'In that case, I shall take the blame for turning up early and seeing the work in progress, and I shall rephrase that.' He gestured around the immaculate room. 'Going on first impressions—and Kelly Argent's spirited defence of you—what you've been doing is far more than mere caretaking.'

The compliment fell sweetly on her bruised self-esteem. It wasn't his fault that she still harboured a degree of resentment that she hadn't been appointed to the position.

'As far as that's concerned, you won't really know how well or how badly I've been doing the job until you've been here a week or two,' she cautioned. 'Apart from anything else, you've probably got your own way of organising things and it's not necessarily the way we've got it set up here.'

'We'll just have to wait and see, then, won't we?' he said easily, then visibly switched into work mode. 'Now, what happens about setting up the case notes for the new patients this morning? Who's responsible for collating their previous histories and test results?' He settled himself against the edge of the blessedly clear desk and crossed his long legs at the ankle, and she had to drag her eyes away from all the lean power on display before she could get her mouth to form sensible words.

'Well, you have a very able secretarial team—'

'Team?' he queried with a blink. 'How many, exactly?'

'Job-sharing,' Leah said with a grin, realising that he was imagining a whole squad of people waiting with fingers poised over computer keys. 'As you know, there's a lot of routine correspondence between the department and the patients' respective GPs and-or referring hospital, all needing to be kept in the loop.'

'A lot?' he echoed with a grimace. 'Make that a mountain of the stuff.'

'Quite!' she agreed with feeling. 'And while it's important that it's all kept up to date, we learned that there was no reason why it had to be done strictly nine to five when there were plenty of people wanting jobs at different times of day—mums with preschoolers who prefer to spend the day with them and work a shift when their partner comes home after work, or mums with school-age children who want to finish in time to be there at the end of school, for example. It was just a matter of putting the pieces of jigsaw together to have enough man-…and woman-power to get the job done.'

He nodded thoughtfully, his eyes never leaving her face.

'And I don't suppose I need to ask who worked the jigsaw out, do I? So, where does this jigsaw live? There certainly isn't room in here.'

'No, and it wouldn't have been workable with patient consultations going on either.' Her sense of the ridiculous kicked in. 'To maintain patient confidentiality, they'd have had to spend a fair amount of time standing outside the door, waiting until it was appropriate to come back in.'

'So?' he prompted, the slight quirk at the corner of his mouth apparently all the humour he was going to allow himself now he was in an 'on duty' frame of mind.

'So there's a small office immediately behind the reception desk as you come into the department,' Leah explained, disappointed that the connection she'd felt between them seemed to have been deliberately severed. Or had she imagined it? 'When you want whoever's on duty to come to your office, you can either pick up the phone to call them in, or stretch your legs with a quick stroll along the corridor. I printed up a list of the various contact codes and taped it to the computer monitor—the side closest to the phone.'

'And are they responsible for organising the patient files each day?' he queried, returning to his original question.

'Yes, and no,' Leah admitted, feeling a twinge of disloyalty towards her old boss, even though she'd despaired of his slapdash methods with paperwork. 'Donald hated anyone "*messing*" with the files. He liked keeping the current ones "to hand" as he called it, but he didn't really have a system.'

'Hmm. At a guess, the only reason why he could find the file he was looking for was because you'd put it right under his hand,' he suggested wryly. 'So, what system had you devised for yourself over the last few months?'

'A simple one,' she said, and couldn't help the grin that went with the announcement, especially when it made that fugitive smile reappear on his face. She had to deliberately ignore the increase in her pulse rate that it caused, silently reminding herself that he was her new boss and they were here to work.

'Because I was doing the audit, I've been getting out each day's files myself, but there's no reason why they can't be got ready for you at the start of the day now. Here, let me show you,' she offered, and proceeded to unlock the rest of the cabinets and the deceptive cupboard door behind which was hidden a handbasin and shelves neatly stacked with disposable supplies.

Because she'd devised the system, it didn't take long for her to point out the way she'd organised everything, including her favourite drawers—the ones with the files of the department's most recent successes, many with photographs of those precious successes.

'Actually,' she began hesitantly, 'I was thinking of putting up a board somewhere in the department with all the photos on it—a sort of positive reinforcement for the parents going through the mill at the moment.'

'You haven't already got one?' he said with a frown, settling himself back against the desk and endangering her concentration again. 'I'm sure I've seen some photos...'

'Oh, there *are* photos around,' she agreed quickly, wondering what on earth was the matter with her. She'd never been one to ogle men's bodies, yet here she was, hardly able to drag her eyes away from him. 'Some mums and dads send us photos, and others actually come back to visit and then we get Kelly's instant camera out. The results are scattered on various walls, but I thought it might be a good idea if we could—'

'Of course we should!' he exclaimed. 'I can't imagine why there isn't one already.'

'I don't think Donald could see the point of spending the time on it. He wasn't really interested in his surroundings.' Leah didn't know why she felt it necessary to explain. His successor already had the memory of the drab room he'd inherited to go on.

'So where were you suggesting we put this photo collection? In here?' He straightened up from the desk and turned around in a circle. 'There's a stretch of blank wall there, over the filing cabinets.'

'Either that, or the big wall that confronts you as you come into the AR department,' she suggested.

'Or both?' he countered. 'This wall for our patients to see during their consultations, but the other one can be seen by everyone who visits Obs and Gyn when they get a glimpse of it through the glass doors. There's nothing like a display of baby photos to put a smile on your face.'

'Except when you're one of those who *can't* have one of their own, no matter how sophisticated the technology,' Leah pointed out sombrely. 'Then it can just be another source of heartbreak.'

'It can be devastating,' he agreed quietly, 'Especially when they've pinned all their hopes on us helping them. Too many think that IVF is the absolute answer—that they're guaranteed success just by coming here and going through the system. They don't realise just how many women…and men…there are for whom we can do nothing.'

Leah knew the statistics only too well, having been a part of them. 'It's especially hard when there's absolutely no apparent reason for the failure,' she added, and when he sharpened his gaze on her, she wondered if her own devastation had been evident in her voice.

She held her breath for a second, hoping that he wouldn't ask. There was no way she could talk to him about it—no way she could talk to anyone without becoming emotional about her failure.

'All we can do is keep trying to find reasons and means to get around them and, in the meantime, do our best for as many as we can,' he said, and she started breathing again.

'Now!' he said briskly, standing and gesturing towards the door. 'If you would like to lead the way, I think it would be a good idea if you introduced me to the first pieces of my jigsaw puzzle before the patients start arriving.'

'What about the nursing and ancillary staff?' she

suggested. 'Do you want me to get everybody together so you can have a quick word?'

'No, thank you!' he said with a definite shudder. 'The last thing I want to do is the "rally the troops" scene. I'd far rather meet them a few at a time so that we can get to know each other. I want them to know that I'm approachable—in fact, I insist on it. If there's something a member of my staff wants to tell me, or ask me, the last thing they need is a remote figure-head.'

'Message received and understood!' Leah feigned a salute but her heart was growing lighter by the minute when she realised just how different the department was going to be under its new head. Obviously, it wasn't as satisfying as if she'd been appointed, but the situation could have been much worse. Now all she needed was an hour or three to work out what went wrong with her pulse every time he looked at her with those stunning blue-green eyes. 'I'll certainly pass the word around that you're happy for people to—'

'What do you mean, *pass the word*?' he interrupted, stopping and turning back so suddenly that she nearly ended up with her nose pressed to his pristine white shirt…and the broad chest beneath it… Her unruly pulse went into overdrive again.

She took a hasty step back, but it still wasn't far enough to escape the enticing mixture of soap and man that surrounded them.

'You're going to be coming with me,' he continued, apparently completely oblivious to her turmoil, thank goodness. 'I'm going to be relying on you to perform the introductions as we go.'

So much for getting a chance to catch my breath, she thought as she directed him along the corridor with a wave of one shaky hand. It sounded as if she was going to be working all too closely with the man for at least the next few days. There certainly wasn't going to be time to analyse the effect he was having on her.

CHAPTER FOUR

'LEAH? Can I have a word?' queried a hesitant voice.

Leah looked up from the mountain of paperwork on her newly acquired desk and saw the petite figure of one of the department's team of secretaries hovering in the evening shadows outside the doorway.

'Of course you can, Sue. Come in.' She groaned as she straightened her back. 'Anything to take a break from this. I swear I'm going to end up hunchbacked before my next birthday. Is there a problem?'

'My husband just rang. He said that my daughter—Mandy, she's three—has just been very sick and she's crying for me. I wondered if you wouldn't mind...'

'Of course you should go home to her,' Leah said immediately. 'Apart from the fact that Mandy needs her mum, you've often worked on when we've needed you to in the past so it's only fair.'

'Are you sure? It won't cause problems with David that I haven't finished all the typing, will it?'

'I'm positive. Now, scoot! And give her a cuddle for me.'

Sue thanked her breathlessly then hurried away, home to the husband and child waiting for her.

'While *I* might just as well stay here all night,' Leah muttered with a burst of uncharacteristic despondency. 'My bonsai certainly aren't waiting to be tucked up for the night.'

The echo of her words came back to her and when

she realised just how self-pitying and downright silly they sounded, she shook her head and got back to work.

She didn't know how long she'd been concentrating and hadn't really registered the fact that she was totally alone at this far end of the department. It happened so often and had never mattered before...until she heard the sound of footsteps coming along the corridor towards the office.

She froze with her hands suspended over the computer keyboard, every hair on her body lifting as her skin tightened with fear.

There was someone else in the department with her and there shouldn't be, not now that Sue had gone home. Had she been in such a hurry to get to her daughter that she hadn't checked that the door had shut properly behind her?

The only time this department was humming with noise and movement was when their patients arrived for consultations. Any procedures—and the babies that hopefully resulted from them—took place at the other end of the obs and gyn floor. *That* was staffed twenty-four hours a day, and as she was first on call tonight, if they'd needed her to assist with a difficult delivery, someone would have paged her rather than wasting time coming for her on foot.

Now it was almost eerily silent except for the owner of those feet, and whoever it was definitely shouldn't be here.

A flurry of scenarios whirled through her head like autumn leaves in a high wind...

Had someone broken into the department in search of drugs?

Was it a stalker, seeing her lonely light and picking her out as an easy, isolated target?

It couldn't be Sue returning to work. She wouldn't be back until her next scheduled shift and, anyway, these footsteps sounded far more like a man's.

Even as she concentrated on the way they were drawing ever closer to her door, their pace slowed and grew ominously quiet.

Her heartbeat didn't. It was working so hard to pump the adrenaline around her system that she was surprised the walls weren't vibrating in time with its mad gallop.

Then the door was flung open so suddenly that she gave a shriek of shock, her knees trembling too much for her to get out of her chair, never mind running.

'Leah! I thought you were an intruder. What on earth are *you* doing here?' David demanded harshly as he stalked into the room.

'I work here,' she snapped back, too shaken to say more.

'Not at this time of night,' he declared, abruptly leaning over her shoulder to press buttons on the keyboard.

With a blink of amazement she watched him save what she'd been doing and shut the programme down as efficiently as if he'd been using the system for years rather than a single day.

'You've done too much overtime in the last weeks and months,' he continued, taking a scant step back before swivelling her chair to face him. 'You've essentially been running the department single-handedly, and then you threw in a marathon decorating spree. You should be home, catching up on some sleep.'

He reached out both hands and her thoughts were so jumbled that she automatically put her own in them. Effortlessly, he pulled her to her feet, only to have to grab her and pull her against him for support when her shaky knees refused to bear her weight.

'Hey! Are you all right? Are you ill?' he demanded, peering down at her face, and those stunning eyes met hers at close quarters, robbing her of what little breath she had left.

She'd forgotten just how good this could feel, she thought as she registered the supporting way he'd wrapped his arms around her, surrounding her with his strength and his warmth. She felt safe, here…almost cherished.

But that was crazy!

She'd only known the man a matter of days, and now that she thought about it…

She stiffened and pushed herself away from him, refusing to acknowledge that she missed the physical contact.

'No thanks to you!' she snapped. 'What are you doing, stomping around at this time of night? Storming in here like that could have given me a heart attack.'

'Only if you had a serious heart problem to begin with,' he pointed out far too rationally. He folded his arms across his chest and leant back against the desk in an increasingly familiar stance. 'And the reason why I came in like that was to surprise whoever was in here, interfering with the medical records.'

'Interfering with records?'

'Well, it's not as if there's anything else of value in here. The computer's hardly top of the line and for all your hard work redecorating, the fixtures and fittings certainly aren't worth risking a gaol sentence to steal. In fact,' he said, warming to his theme, '*you're* probably the most valuable item in the room, *and* the most at risk if there were an intruder.'

'Oh, that's crazy,' she protested.

'It's not crazy at all, when you think of all the statistics about hospital staff being attacked. In fact, I
don't want you staying on your own in the department
at night. When you're in this office, you're far too far
away for anyone to hear if you needed help.'

Leah wasn't feeling frightened any more. In fact,
her blood was boiling that he thought he could hand
out such high-handed commands.

'And how am I supposed to do my job if I'm banned
from the department?' she demanded heatedly. 'How
am I supposed to keep all my paperwork up to date?
What am I supposed to do with myself if I'm on call—
sit and twiddle my thumbs and drink too much coffee
instead of getting on with things?' She planted one fist
on each hip, determined to stand her ground. 'This is
nothing more than blatant sex discrimination. We
wouldn't even be having this discussion if I were a
man.'

'You're partly right about that,' he agreed calmly,
his level voice only infuriating her more. 'But until
Maintenance has been around the department beefing
up security, that's the way it's going to be. I will not
be responsible for putting members of staff at risk.'

'You *wouldn't* be responsible,' she snapped. 'It's *my*
choice to work on in the evening and I've been responsible for my own actions for a good few years
now. My decisions and my safety are my own respon-
sibility.'

'Fine!' he agreed abruptly, but before she could sa-
vour the fact that he'd backed down he added, 'As
long as you realise that you'd also be responsible for
blowing a hole in the AR department's meagre budget.
If you insist on staying, I'll have to pay for someone

from Security to sit outside the door until you go home.'

'What! That's ridiculous!' There was absolutely nothing wrong with her knees as she stomped across the limited space in the room to stand almost nose to nose with him, conscious that she must sound like a fishwife. 'There's no reason to have anyone sitting outside the door. I've been working alone in the department for months and there's never been any problem. I don't see why—'

'Because I said so,' he cut in brutally, then paused and groaned. 'Did you hear what I just said? You've got me using those dreadful phrases my parents used to say, and I always swore I'd never do it.'

'And it's hardly appropriate as I'm not your child,' she pointed out stiffly. 'You can't tell me what I can—'

'I'm head of department,' he broke in very softly, not a trace of levity in his voice this time. He was obviously deadly serious. 'I had a look around the department earlier today and discovered just how many roundabout routes there are to access this particular floor, so until Maintenance have sorted out the security, I will be making an absolute rule that *no one* stays here on their own.'

Leah had never really thought about the fact that there was more than one staircase and more than one bank of lifts accessing the obs and gyn floor. If she was honest, she could remember hearing the sound of approaching feet just a few minutes ago and the way her heart had pounded while she'd wondered if Sue had forgotten to shut the door properly on her way out. If it *hadn't* been David...

'How long is it all going to take?' she demanded,

finally conceding that this was a battle she wasn't going to win. 'I hope you realise that it can take months to get even simple repairs done.'

She dreaded the thought of getting behind with her work. It had nearly killed her to have to spend so many hours sorting out Donald's neglected filing. She certainly didn't want to have to do it all over again. She also couldn't bear the idea that someone might miss their last window of opportunity for having a family of their own if she didn't keep on top of every detail.

'They promised that it would be done before the end of the week,' he announced, and she blinked in surprise.

'Did they say *which* week?' she asked skeptically, and surprised half a grin out of him. She was taken aback to discover that it actually felt good to make him smile, sending an unexpected warmth spiralling through her.

'*This* week,' he confirmed with a roll of his eyes. 'Now, is there anything you need to pick up before I see you home?'

'See me home?' It was her turn to smile. It was years since anyone had offered to see her home. It was almost a shame that she didn't need him to. 'I came by car.'

'In that case, I'll see you to your car.'

'Phil or Den usually do that,' she pointed out, and at his frown explained, 'The night security men on the main door. They take it in turn to keep an eye on the female staff until they're safely in their cars.'

She paused in the hallway while he checked that the office door had closed properly behind them then had to hurry to keep up with his much longer strides.

'Sorry,' he muttered when he realised what was happening. 'I forgot you're small.'

'I'm not small for a woman,' she objected as the lift doors opened and he gestured for her to enter. 'In fact, if I'd been an inch taller I could have been a model.'

'Did you want to be a model?' He seemed intrigued by the idea but the way his eyes gleamed as they roamed over her from head to toe suddenly made the steel-walled lift feel more like a sauna.

'I've heard it's exhausting and boring but I've heard that the pay is fantastic for the most successful, and, no, I'd never want to be a model even if I did have the height.'

The doors slid open again on the ground floor, partly masking his muttered comment. It had actually sounded as if he'd said, 'You've got all the rest of the equipment.' But that couldn't be right. She'd never had the right equipment—at least, not in working order.

She threw him a frowning glance and instantly knew she must have been mistaken. His thoughts were clearly elsewhere than on her dubious charms, especially when the first thing he spoke about when the lift doors closed was the work she'd been doing on the computer.

'I take it you were entering the details of the latest batch of new patients?'

'And starting all the new cross-checks to verify their identities,' she confirmed. 'Although I can't say I feel very comfortable with the process.'

'Neither am I,' he said grimly. 'When you're dealing with people desperate to have a child, it doesn't seem right to waste precious time playing the policeman to check up that they're telling the truth.

Unfortunately there are sound reasons why the rules and regulations are set down.'

'Not least the fact that multiple births have a far higher incidence of birth defects, with fewer surviving, and that older mums have a pitifully low rate of success with a greater chance of complications. Yes, I know all that, but it still feels…wrong, somehow, to have to pry into every nook and cranny before we can make a final decision.'

'You'll find it feels much less *wrong*—' he deliberately stressed her own word '—if you think of it from the other direction. You're doing the checks to make absolutely sure that you're giving any babies the best possible chance. After all, they're the reason why we're doing all this.'

'At least we don't have to make the final decisions all by ourselves,' she muttered as she watched the numbers change above the doors. 'We can blame ''the committee'' if we have to pass on bad news.'

David was just waving a signal to the security man on duty—Den tonight, Leah registered—indicating that he was going to escort Leah to her car, when both their pagers started to shrill.

'Oops!' Leah performed her about-face a second faster than David did and ended up ploughing into him…again!

For just a fraction of a second she forgot to be embarrassed and simply enjoyed the feel of such a solidly male body against hers. Then his long legs were taking him rapidly in the direction of the lifts and there was no time for such nonsensical imaginings.

'Can you tell Obs and Gyn we're on our way?' Leah called over her shoulder, and Den waved a hand in acknowledgement, his other hand already reaching for the phone.

This time she was still filled with a strange awareness of every breath David took as they stood watching the numbers above the door, but there was an overriding impatience to reach their destination and find out what emergency necessitated both of them to attend.

Yin Bo Chan was waiting for them when the lift doors swished open and blinked, apparently surprised to see the two of them arrive together.

'What's the problem?' David demanded as he strode towards her, already taking the cufflinks out of his shirt ready to don protective clothing. Leah was left to hurry in his wake.

'Oh, dear! You're both here!' exclaimed the petite midwife. 'I only asked for whoever was on call.'

'That's me,' Leah announced. 'How can I help?'

'Actually,' David interrupted, 'I replaced your name on the board tonight. I put myself as first on call, so you could catch up on some sleep.'

'Well, as you forgot to tell me...' Leah said ominously, her anger at his high-handedness returning in full force. She turned back to the increasingly uncomfortable midwife. 'Did you have a problem?'

'One of your IVF patients, Mrs Joliffe, has presented with antepartum haemorrhage and pain.'

Leah's heart sank at the news. After years of misery, Pam Joliffe was finally, ecstatically pregnant.

'How many weeks is she?' David demanded, just beating Leah to the punch. In spite of the fact that she'd been so recently updating all the patient files, she couldn't immediately recall the stage the pregnancy had reached. If it was too soon for viability...

'She's thirty-three weeks gestation with twins,' Yin

said succinctly. 'She's in pain but there's no rigidity to the belly. No apparent contractions, but the cervix is slightly dilated—less than one centimetre.'

'Yin…?' called a panic-stricken voice in the nearby room, swiftly followed by a head appearing round the door.

Leah fought a sympathetic grin when she recognised Greg Martin, one of the newest recruits to the department, a junior doctor in his first week of a six-month obs and gyn rotation. He looked distinctly green around the gills and was almost quivering with apprehension.

'Oh, hello, sir,' he said over a nervous gulp when he saw who was standing there. He visibly braced himself to make a report. 'We've put Mrs Joliffe on oxygen and put two large-bore cannulae in. So far, she's only on Ringer's solution for hydration. I've taken…' He paused, then corrected himself. 'Actually, *Yin* has taken blood and ordered U and E, FBC, blood glucose, cross-match, rhesus and antibody status, Kleihauer test and clotting screen. We've also got cardiotocography running to monitor the baby and we were just going to do an ultrasound scan to see if the blood loss was part of a much larger haemorrhage retained behind the placenta.'

He was completely out of breath by the time he came to the end of his recitation, and also, rather obviously, feeling totally out of his depth, but Leah couldn't fault any of it.

'Well, done, Greg,' David said quietly, and Leah wasn't surprised to see the steadying effect the praise had on the young man's nerves. Somehow the sincerity of his tone was far more potent than any amount of gushing praise.

'You've made a good start,' he continued, automatically reaching to the nearby dispenser to tip soap into his hands to wash them before he joined their patient. 'Now, what would your next steps be?'

'My next steps?' he repeated faintly.

Leah had to duck her head over her own hand-washing when she heard Greg's loud gulp of apprehension, but she was impressed with David's teaching style. Some consultants were far too quick to take over without giving their juniors a chance to test themselves, even with a verbal run-through of possible courses of action.

'Ah, well... It would partly depend on blood loss and the degree of separation we see on the scan...?' he suggested hesitantly, and at David's encouraging nod expanded on his theme. 'If it shows placental abruption, we'll need to do a Caesarean before the babies get into difficulty, in spite of the fact their lungs aren't mature enough yet. If there's no major abruption, we continue support and see if things settle down enough to go closer to term.'

'Well, then, let's go in and see our patient. When we see what's on the scan, we can make our decision,' David said with a smile and a gesture for Greg to lead the way.

Our patient...and *we* can make a decision, he'd said, and as she followed the two of them into the room, Leah couldn't help noticing that, thanks to David's careful choice of words and his encouraging manner, the young man seemed to have grown at least an inch taller in the last few minutes and he wasn't nearly as pale and shaky any more.

'Oh, no!' exclaimed Pam Joliffe fearfully when she

saw the three of them arriving. 'What's happened to my babies?'

'Nothing, as far as we know,' soothed David. 'Whatever makes you think something's wrong?'

'So many of you arriving at once,' she said anxiously. 'It *must* be bad news.'

David laughed easily, as if he hadn't a care in the world.

'No,' he said. 'That's just called bad planning on our part. I'm David ffrench, the new head of department, and Dr Dawson and I had just finished a meeting when our pagers went off. Dr Martin knew that one of us would want to see you as you're one of our special patients. Anyway, we decided that it was far too undignified to have an argument in the middle of Reception about whose turn it was to come up, so we both came to see you together.'

His apparently light-hearted manner took some of the panic out of Pam's expression and her tension eased still further when he perched himself on the edge of her bed.

Leah wondered if she was the only one who noticed that he started to reach for her hand, only to cover the gesture by curling his own into a loose fist and resting it on his thigh.

Was it the new politically correct regulations about unnecessary physical contact between patient and caregiver that had prompted the withdrawal? Leah didn't know, but the fact that he'd had to consciously stop himself from automatically offering the comfort of human touch told her a great deal about the type of doctor he was, and her chagrin about losing the job to him faded a little more.

'Now, what have you been up to?' he asked gently.

'I think you're in too much of a hurry to meet these little people. I'd rather they stayed where they are to cook a little longer.'

'I wasn't doing anything silly, I promise, especially with my husband away,' she said, suddenly tearful as she threw a pleading glance towards Leah. '*You* know how long it's taken me to get this far in a pregnancy. I wouldn't do *anything* to jeopardise…' She couldn't finish.

'We know you wouldn't,' Leah said soothingly. 'But if you remember, I did warn you that twins often try to arrive early, probably because carrying two is an extra burden on the mother's reserves. What Dr Martin's going to do now is run a few checks to see whether the two of them really mean it, or if we can persuade them to stay put a bit longer.'

Out of the corner of her eye she could see the ultrasound trolley being wheeled into position and she stepped aside, carefully positioning herself so that she'd be able to see the screen without getting in the way.

It was a relief to see the shadowy images of first one and then the other baby, and she was nearly as relieved as the mother when those images showed both strongly beating hearts much in evidence.

The rest of the news wasn't quite as rosy, as the screen displayed images of a definite area of separation of one placenta from the uterus.

Pam was unaware of the problem and was now sobbing with relief that her precious babies were still alive and well. She was delighted when she was offered printed copies of the clearest images of their faces.

Leah was loath to puncture her euphoria but a glance at the concerned frown pleating David's forehead confirmed the necessity. He looked up to meet her waiting gaze and without a word needing to be spoken, she knew what the decision had to be.

She had a horrible feeling about this one, but it was the strange sensation of connection she'd had when their eyes had met that was worrying her more. She barely knew the man and there was absolutely no point in developing any sort of relationship between them apart from a professional one.

'Pam, I want to start you on some steroid injections,' David announced calmly, dragging her besotted eyes away from the pictures and Leah's attention back to the job in hand.

'Steroids?' she echoed, clearly puzzled. 'What for? Aren't they what athletes use to cheat in their races…or is it what body-builders take to pump up their muscles?'

'Both, unfortunately,' David confirmed. 'They take anabolic steroids and, because they take them in excess, they can do untold long-term damage to their bodies. In your case, we want to give you corticosteroids—just a short course over a couple of days—to help the babies' lungs to mature.'

'Why do you need to do that?' Panic was creeping in again and she briefly clutched the pictures protectively to her chest before gazing at them with renewed fear. 'The pictures show that they're all right…don't they?'

'Your babies are beautiful and strong, but the pictures also showed us that there's an area of one of the placentas that's coming "unglued" from your uterus,' he explained gently. 'That's why you were bleeding.'

'But the bleeding's stopped now, hasn't it?' she implored. 'Everything's going to be all right, isn't it?'

'We hope so,' he agreed. 'But we don't want to leave anything to chance, either with the babies' health or with yours. That's why we want to give you the steroids.'

'But what will they do?' she demanded. 'Glue the placenta back again?'

'We wish it was that easy,' Leah said with a chuckle that she hoped would lighten the fraught atmosphere a little. It failed.

'We're hoping that everything will settle down,' David continued, 'but just in case we have to deliver the babies early, the steroids help to make their lungs stronger, so it isn't quite so much of a shock when they have to start breathing much earlier than they should.'

'Oh, God!' she wailed. 'Why is this all happening when Jonty's so far away? When they're submerged, I can't even phone him and get him to come home.'

'Submerged?' Greg echoed, clearly puzzled.

'He's a Royal Navy submariner,' Leah explained in a succinct aside, leaving the younger man to work out the logistics of getting a man out of a vessel deep under one of the world's oceans at short notice and transporting him to his wife's bedside.

'He'd already organised to take some leave so he could be with me when the babies are due,' Pam continued tearfully. 'If anything happens *now*, it could take *days* before they could get him here.'

'Well, that gives us time to make sure that this pair are in the best possible health when he does finally make it,' Leah said, deliberately upbeat.

'On the plus side, there's the fact that you've only had a bleed,' Greg offered.

'Only? What do you mean, *only*?' The panic was back in full measure and Leah had to stifle a groan.

'Oh…well…' *Now* Greg realised his mistake and glanced across in a mute appeal for help out of the hole he'd just dug under his own feet.

'You really don't want to have to listen to a long and boring lecture on obstetrics and gynaecology,' Leah said quickly, hoping to distract Pam, 'especially when we already know that your babies aren't growing two heads apiece, have all the right number of arms and legs and have fully functioning circulatory systems.'

Above all, she didn't want Greg to mention the fact that they were all crossing their fingers that she wouldn't start having contractions. Ritodrine would be their drug of choice to halt labour and could buy them a little more time, but it wasn't suitable in every case and certainly wouldn't be a guarantee of success.

'How long will I have to be on the steroids?' Pam asked as she watched the intramuscular injection being prepared.

'Just four doses at twelve-hourly intervals,' Yin Bo Chan confirmed soothingly as she smoothed the covers back into position.

'So I have to come back in twelve hours for the next one?' she said with a glance at her watch.

'No, we'll be keeping you in for a while, so that we can keep a close eye on you…and the babies,' David added quickly, certain that concern for her precious children would override any objections. 'It will give you a couple of days to catch up on your sleep and do a bit of reading while someone else does the cooking.'

'But there's still so much left to do to get ready before they arrive,' Pam fretted, still close to tears.

'I've still got the last pieces of furniture to get for the nursery and I haven't finished half of the knitting I was going to do.'

'Well, you can do all the knitting you want in here,' he pointed out. 'And I'm certain your babies won't be critical if their nursery isn't perfectly kitted out. They wouldn't be the first to have to go to sleep in a padded drawer.'

'Well, no, but—'

'But nothing, Pam.' This time David *did* touch her, resting a reassuring hand over hers where her fingers worried the sheet into a series of crumpled pleats. 'No worrying allowed. Leave that to us. All *you* have to do is concentrate on relaxing and getting that knitting done. Sister will be able to ring a friend or neighbour to fetch whatever you need from home.'

Whether it was his touch or his words of reassurance that finally got through to her, Leah didn't know, but he'd achieved his purpose as Pam finally relaxed her head on the pillow.

CHAPTER FIVE

'LET me give you a lift home,' Leah offered when they finally made it to her car an hour later, their patient resigned to spending at least the next few days in hospital for the sake of her babies.

Once more, David had insisted on walking her across the car park, their shadows impossibly long under the security lights, but all Leah had been able to think about was how good it felt to have his company for the short walk.

It definitely didn't feel the same when Phil or Den accompanied her. There wasn't the same awareness of the scant inches between David's arm and hers as they'd crossed the reception area, or her reaction to his brief touch at the small of her back as he'd ushered her through the door into the chill of the night outside.

'Thanks for the offer, but there's no need. I don't live far enough away to warrant it,' he said, nodding in the direction of the block of flats just outside the hospital grounds. 'I've just moved into Cedars.'

'Cedars,' she echoed stupidly, as if she didn't know the name of her own address, then several half-forgotten facts suddenly connected. '*You're* the person who moved into the top-floor flat the other day.' She'd been working when the removals company had delivered his belongings but until this moment had had no idea whether the new owner had moved in with them. No wonder she hadn't caught sight of her new neighbour if he'd been spending all his time at the hospital.

'How could you know where I…?' He didn't bother finishing his question, so something in her face must have told him the answer. 'You live in the same block,' he said with a wry smile. 'In that case, it makes sense to accept your offer…although I'm surprised you thought it worthwhile to drive such a short distance.' He strode round to the passenger side and opened the door as soon as she activated the key fob to release the locks, and she had to grit her teeth to prevent the heated words spilling out before she'd had time to temper them.

She managed to wait until he'd fastened his safety belt before she refuted what she saw as an unwarranted criticism.

'I drove for exactly the same reason that you escorted me across the car park tonight—because it's safer than walking at this time of the year,' she said sharply, resenting that he seemed to see her as both lazy and wasteful. 'As the evenings grow lighter, I won't bother.'

'Oops!' he said ruefully. 'That was obviously a case of open mouth and insert foot, especially after I'd made such a point of escorting you. And I'm sorry for impugning your conservational tendencies.'

'You're forgiven,' she said with a decidedly gracious nod, surprised that he'd been so quick to admit his mistake and once more fighting the urge to grin. She really didn't want to find the man so…humorous… self-deprecating…appealing. It was bad enough that they were going to be working together, but to discover that they were going to be living together…

No! Not living together!

Just the thought of the words filled her imagination with forbidden images.

What she'd meant was that they were going to be living in the same building, and the fact that there was going to be nothing more than a single, far-from-soundproof wall separating their flats made it doubly important that she stamped hard on any feelings of attraction towards him. That would be a certain recipe for disaster.

It wasn't a long journey around the hospital's perimeter road and out of the main gates and then it was just a matter of yards before she turned into the parking area attached to the small block of flats, but Leah clamped her mouth shut, determined not to allow any further conversation to build between the two of them. If she was going to react so strongly to the man after such a short acquaintance—it was just the fact that she'd discovered that he was going to be living in the same block of flats, for heaven's sake—then she was going to have to work harder than ever to stop her emotions becoming involved.

So, having made that decision, why did she find herself pausing outside her front door, the key already in her hand, ready to make her escape behind the safety of solid wood?

'Would you like something to drink?' she heard herself say, and nearly groaned aloud. That certainly wasn't the way to maintain some distance between the two of them. 'Not coffee, of course…not if we want to get to sleep…'

If we want to get to sleep? As she realised that she'd made it sound as if the two of them would be sleeping together, her face flamed with embarrassment and she tried to cover her gaffe with hurried words. 'I've got tea or fruit juice or bottled water or—'

'I'm still unpacking,' David said, and she breathed a sigh of relief that he was actually going to let her off the hook, then he dashed her hopes when he added, 'and I didn't manage to get to the shops today either, so I'd love a cup of tea.'

Silently damning her unruly tongue she slid the key into the lock and swung the door open then led the way inside.

This was the last thing she'd needed, she thought as she flipped on each light as she passed on her way to the tiny kitchen, overwhelmingly aware of the steady footsteps behind her that told her he was following her.

She had to see him at the hospital every day and now that she knew he lived in the same building she could expect to run into him here from time to time, but at least her flat could have been a ffrench-free zone.

Not any more. With her invitation, she now wouldn't be able to relax without seeing the way he propped one shoulder against the door-frame while he watched her fill the kettle, those stunning blue-green eyes seeming to follow her every move as she hovered over the choice between proper cups or her usual mugs.

'A mug is fine for me,' he murmured. 'I don't take sugar, so I won't need a saucer to put the spoon in.'

Leah wasn't certain if she was comfortable with the way he seemed to be able to read her mind. She hadn't realised that she was that transparent, she thought as she retrieved the milk from the fridge, then paused as she caught sight of the food neatly stacked in her fridge.

She might have been busy, but she hadn't been trying to move house at the same time, she argued silently
as she justified the urge to give the man something to
eat. She certainly hadn't seen him leave the department
for anything as mundane as a trip to the canteen and
she'd be surprised if he'd had anything more than coffee all day. He must be starving.

'Do you subscribe to the theory that real men don't
eat quiche?' she challenged as she withdrew a thick
wedge filled to the brim with bacon and cheese and
topped with colourful circles of tomato and placed it
on the work surface in full sight.

For a second he seemed startled into silence as his
eyes travelled from the food to her almost combative
stance, then his face creased into a grin that completely
stole her breath.

'Actually, I subscribe to the theory that real men
will eat anything they can get their hands on if they
want to keep body and soul together,' he admitted.
'Especially something that looks as good as that.
Anything's better than chicken ping.'

'Chicken *ping*?' she echoed, sidetracked by the un-
familiar phrase.

'Anything heated in the microwave,' he explained
with a grimace. 'It doesn't seem to matter what fancy
name they give it on the packet, it all tastes the same.'

'As well as being woefully short on protein and
massively overloaded with salt and artificial colourings
and flavourings,' she agreed. 'Well, give me a second
to pour your tea and then you can take your mug into
the other room while I get some salad out to go with
the quiche.'

'If I sit down, I'll probably be asleep before you can
get it on a plate,' he admitted wryly, then began to roll

up his sleeves. 'Put me to work instead. Which would you rather I did—pour the tea or make the salad?'

'Oh, but...' That had backfired with a vengeance, she thought with a silent groan. She'd suggested he wait in the other room to put a bit of distance between them and give her a chance to get her galloping pulse to settle down. Now they were going to be in closer proximity than ever in her tiny kitchen.

'If you pour the tea, then,' she conceded weakly as she busied herself at the fridge again, retrieving a selection from the salad drawer in the bottom.

Over the next few minutes she was still very aware of every move he made but there was that strange feeling of companionship and uniformity of purpose as they prepared the meal together that she'd had right from the first time they'd worked together to deliver that unexpected set of IVF triplets.

That reminded her...

'Did you hear that the last of the Masson triplets is breathing on his own?' she asked over the muted clatter of cutlery being added to the tray.

'Yes. Isn't it great? If he continues to do this well, his sister will soon be able to come back to join them,' David said with a smile. 'I must say, I was horrified when I realised she was going to have to be sent halfway across the country to another unit because we didn't have room for her.'

'It doesn't happen often,' Leah said defensively, even though she knew the system was indefensible and one that she'd railed against herself. 'It's only when we have an unexpected multiple birth when we're already full of highly dependent babies, or when we have an urgent referral from one of the hospitals that doesn't have a specialist unit like ours. Then we have to free up a bed by sending the strongest one here to the nearest bed that can cope with their needs.'

'It just seems crazy to me,' he said heatedly. 'We've got all the equipment and the expertise of a centre of excellence but we're having to turn away babies from other hospitals and even send away babies that are already here—risking their lives in unnecessary ambulance journeys—just because there aren't enough qualified staff available for that level of high-dependence nursing.'

'Well, if you can think of some way to get the bone-heads at the top to realise that unless you pay them a proper wage, love of the job alone won't keep staff in the department...' Leah knew she didn't have to complete the sentence. It seemed as if it was an almost worldwide complaint that dedication to a profession was no guarantee of appreciation by the paymasters. 'Still, now that you've been appointed, perhaps you can do some cage rattling,' she suggested over her shoulder. 'Donald hated all the politics involved. He just liked getting on with the job.'

She turned to face him with a plate in each hand. 'I hope you like potato salad, as well as green. I had some leftovers to use up.'

It made her feel good to see the way his eyes lit up at the colourful display on the plate she held out to him.

For just a moment she allowed herself to remember how much she'd enjoyed the daily rituals of being half of a couple—all the little companionable gestures and intimacies, the caring—then quickly pushed the memories away. There was no point in yearning after them because there was no chance of ever experiencing them again, not when she knew how it would inevitably end.

'You didn't have to do this,' he demurred, then added hastily, 'not that I don't appreciate it, because I do. How on earth did you manage to whip all this up so quickly?'

It was flattering how eagerly he settled himself at the table to take the first mouthful and the appreciative groans that followed were almost sexual.

Don't go there! she told herself sternly when her atrophied hormones began to sit up and take notice.

'The green salad doesn't take more than a minute,' she said, hastily dragging her thoughts back to his question—anything to get them away from the possibility of putting her boss and sex in the same image. 'And I cheated with the potato salad because I used bought mayonnaise rather than making my own.'

'And the quiche?' he managed between hearty bites. 'This certainly doesn't look like a commercial product, neither does it taste like it.'

His praise spread a warm glow through her. How long had it been since someone had appreciated her for anything other than her medical skills?

'Thank you for the compliment.' She hoped she wasn't grinning like an idiot. 'I've always enjoyed cooking. I find it's a good way to unwind after a difficult shift.'

'I'm surprised you've had the time since Donald died.' He held up a hand when she would have interrupted. 'I know you aren't the only member of staff—we've got a couple of excellent junior registrars on board and the nursing staff is the equal of any I've worked with—but you were the most senior and by all accounts you'd essentially been running the department for months before Donald went. That was an enormous load, especially when you were short of senior staff.'

Leah was sure her face must be glowing with the heat that poured into it, and it wasn't just David's words. The expression in his eyes told of his sincerity, too, and was there also a hint of personal appreciation, or was that just wishful thinking on her part?

Wishful thinking? Now wait a minute! She pulled her thoughts up short, angry with where they were straying. She didn't want...didn't *need* a man's approval to know she was doing a good job. And she certainly didn't need a man in her life, no matter how tall dark and handsome he was, and certainly not when his eyes held as many shadows as David's did.

With that stern reminder she applied herself to her own meal, using the food as an excuse for ending any attempt at conversation. And the sooner they finished, the sooner he'd stop invading her privacy.

Except when he'd cleared his plate he sat back and started looking at his surroundings and her discomfort increased.

She knew what her flat looked like—almost bereft of furniture since she'd come out of her divorce with little more than her clothing. Since then she'd put all her energies into her career, not bothering with any of the trendy decorating knick-knacks that would make the flat look more homely or more elegant or even more lived in.

'I like this,' he pronounced after a minute, much to her surprise. 'It's totally uncluttered and...peaceful.'

'That's a polite way of saying empty,' she said with a wry grimace. 'Ever since I moved in here, I don't seem to have had time to do anything with it.' Or the inclination, she realised. After all, it was nothing more than somewhere to lay her head at the end of the day. It was never going to be the family home she'd once looked forward to.

'No. I mean it,' he insisted. 'So many of these designer make-overs seem more interested in the high-priced labels they can stuff into a room rather than the…the feeling you get when you're in it. Oh…!' He made a dismissive noise. 'I'm not explaining myself very well, but…look at what you've done in here. There's the minimum of comfortable-looking furniture with enough storage to hide any clutter, and instead of fussy floral arrangements that drop all their petals the day after you buy them, you've got a single plant.'

'Bonsai,' she murmured distractedly as she gazed around at the room anew. Seeing it through his eyes was a revelation because it did look good, far better than she'd realised.

'Bonsai?' he echoed. 'One of those Japanese miniature trees? Didn't I read somewhere that they don't make very good house-plants?'

'You're quite right. The majority only do well outdoors, where they belong, but most will put up with limited stays inside, provided their requirements for light and water are met. Of course, there are some varieties—the ones native to more tropical regions—that can be kept indoors, but their life span is far more precarious because they're prone to… Oh, I'm sorry for rabbiting on like that. Information overload?'

'It's obviously something that interests you.' Those beautiful eyes looked more blue than green this evening and he was watching her as though fascinated by this new facet of her life.

'I visited a Japanese garden several years ago, during a particularly…difficult time.' A time when she'd actually been wondering whether to abandon her career and retrain for something else entirely. 'I was walking through a little bamboo grove and sat down on a bench and an elderly Japanese gentleman started talking to me about listening to the sound of the wind…' She still went back to visit Itsuo Sugiyama whenever she could, especially when the chaos in her life started to overwhelm her. There was something about his timeless view of life that calmed both her mind and spirit.

In between those visits, she had her precious trees to keep her feet on the ground and soothe her heart—not that she would be telling David that. That was something strictly between herself and her trees.

'Well, my place is still half-full of boxes, but if I'm lucky, the washing machine will be connected tomorrow so I'll at least be able to have clean clothes for the next week. All I've got to do is remember to do some grocery shopping tomorrow and I stand a fighting chance of surviving.'

As he was speaking he stood up from the table and she was surprised to feel a sudden pang at the realisation that he was going to leave.

'You did the cooking, so let me help with the washing-up,' he offered, beginning to stack their plates.

'You'd do better to go home and unpack another box or two before you grab some sleep,' she suggested, taking the dirty dishes from him. 'These won't take me a moment, and we've both got a frantically busy day tomorrow. There are thirty patients booked into the morning clinic alone.'

He groaned theatrically. 'And that's without the interruptions we'll get if there are any problem deliveries or transfers from other units.' He paused a moment, just inches away from her. His gaze was warm and steady on her as she waited for him to speak and her heart suddenly performed an improvised quickstep. 'Thank you for the meal tonight,' he said seriously. 'I can't tell you how much I appreciate it…and the company.'

For just a moment it looked as if he was going to reach out to her, and her pulse kicked into a rumba beat, but then he turned away.

'I've put myself as first on call,' he announced as he reached the door, holding up a hand to forestall her objection. 'I've put you on for tomorrow, so catch up on your sleep tonight. You might need it if Mrs Joliffe doesn't settle down as we hope.'

'Don't even think it!' Leah exclaimed. 'Those babies need to stay in there as long as possible…but you already know that as well as I do.'

'If we manage to keep them in there long enough to get the course of steroids into them, that'll be one hurdle crossed, but all I allow myself to do is take things one day at a time,' he said quietly, and for some reason she didn't think he was talking solely about his approach to his work.

'How much longer is it likely to be?' Jonty Joliffe asked when he buttonholed Leah on her way down to a consult in A and E a week later.

He'd arrived just over forty-eight hours after his wife had been admitted and had looked completely shattered as he'd been unaware whether their babies had arrived or not. The fact that the course of steroids had been completed meant that the babies' lungs were now better prepared to deal with the outside world, but after a couple of contractions Pam had needed to be put on ritodrine to prevent her going into labour. The possible side-effects of tachycardia and hypotension meant that she was having to stay in hospital.

While Leah knew that the two of them were ecstatic that their babies were still safe, she also knew that neither of them was dealing well with the boredom of Pam's enforced hospital stay.

'Well, the longer they stay put, the better,' Leah began, not wanting to fob the man off but very aware that there was a patient needing her urgent attention on the ground floor. 'She's not thirty-five weeks yet, and while multiple births usually arrive early, she's still some way from—'

'I know all that,' he said impatiently, then closed his eyes and sighed heavily, shaking his head. 'I apologise, Dr Dawson. That was rude, but…well, I was flown home at enormous expense from the other side of the world because the hospital told us that it was an emergency situation and the babies could be born at any minute, and my leave isn't indefinite.'

'I do understand,' Leah assured him. 'But I'm afraid I don't have any answers for you. This is just a case of taking it one day at a time and hoping that the babies will stay where they are until they're as big and as strong as possible and her body is ready for them to be born.'

'But this drug Pam's on—the ritodrine—couldn't that be stopping the labour when she's already reached that point? She had the steroids to help their lungs so—'

'We're monitoring both Pam and the babies to try to get the optimum moment—the moment when the babies have the best chance of survival without the

risks of brain damage and all the other problems pree-
mies can suffer. If there's the slightest chance that
Pam's body has reached the limits of its tolerance,
we'll have those babies out of there so fast that it'll
make your head swim—and that's a promise!' she
added.

She glanced down at her watch and realised that
time was passing too quickly for her to spend any more
time debating the issue with him. Her unknown patient
was more of a priority at the moment.

'I'm sorry... I'm not trying to fob you off, but I've
been called down to Accident and Emergency to have
a look at a pregnant mum who's been injured. If you
need to speak to me again, I'll be back as soon as I
can.'

She paused only long enough to throw him an apol-
ogetic smile before she hurried out of the department
and took to the stairs at a run.

'Leah Dawson, Obs and Gyn,' she panted as she
arrived in A and E seriously out of breath a few moments later. She took a steadying breath, knowing it
wouldn't do the patient any good to think that her condition warranted doctors sprinting to her side. 'You
want me to take a look at a pregnant mum?'

The charge nurse swung round to consult the ubiq-
uitous white board dominating the wall behind him. It
was covered in colour-coded names allocated to the
various treatment areas, and Leah could remember
only too clearly a very similar board during her rotation in A and E during her training...and the fact that
she didn't think there'd been a single day when she'd
seen it empty.

'Yes. She's in...er, no,' he corrected himself apologetically. 'I'm sorry, we did need you, but Mr ffrench is here so he's seeing her.'

Leah swallowed a sudden flash of anger at the realisation that not only had she just wasted her time and energy hurrying all the way down those dozens of stairs, but David hadn't even had the courtesy of letting her know he was going to take over the call.

With a murmured word and resigned shrug of her shoulders, she set off to retrace her steps. There was no point taking her resentment out on the A and E staff. It wasn't their fault that this had happened again. They weren't to know that over the past few days it didn't matter how hard she worked, every time she turned round, her boss was doing her job as well as his own.

She didn't know what his problem was, she thought as she slogged up the next flight of stairs, torturing herself with the unnecessary exercise to give herself a few minutes to try to work out what had gone wrong between them.

It certainly couldn't be the standard of her work. If anything, having someone with his clinical skills around was lifting the whole department to greater heights. There was almost a buzz in the very air—something that had been sadly lacking in Donald's time.

All she knew was that his strange behaviour seemed to have started the day after she'd invited him into her flat and given him an impromptu meal.

Had he had second thoughts about the implied intimacy of it?

Did he think she'd been chasing after him?

Was he trying to send her a signal that he didn't

want any sort of a relationship between them beyond a professional one?

If that was the case, all he had to do was tell her, and she could reassure him in no uncertain terms that he certainly wasn't so much of a catch that she was willing to change her plans for him. Her plans for her own life couldn't be changed because she didn't have a choice.

She'd more or less talked herself into a more equable frame of mind by the time she pushed open the door at the top of the stairwell, but the first thing she saw as she entered the department was David ffrench exiting the lift and her ire returned full force.

'If you need me, I'll be in Theatre with an emergency Caesarean,' he said brusquely, and was just beginning to stride away from her when Sally Ling appeared in the doorway of Pam Joliffe's room.

'David, the ritodrine's not working any more,' she announced. 'Pam's starting to dilate. Is it worth trying terbutaline?'

If the situation hadn't been so serious, Leah would have laughed at the expression on the head of department's face. For all that he'd been working as hard as a one-armed paper-hanger, he'd finally come up against a situation that he couldn't solve just by working himself harder. There was no way that he could perform an emergency Caesarean at the same time as monitor the state of premature IVF twins.

'David?' she prompted, and for the first time in days he actually met her gaze. What she hadn't expected was to see the fleeting expression of misery in their blue-green depths.

In spite of the rigid control she kept over her own emotions, her heart went out to him. Although he did his best to hide it, this wasn't the first time she'd caught a glimpse of the evidence that something was making him very unhappy.

At the moment there wasn't time to do more than promise herself that she would corner him and demand some answers before too long. Their patients came first.

'Shall I check on Pam while you get started in Theatre?' she suggested. 'As soon as I see what's happening, I'll come through and tell you. If the twins need to be delivered, they can follow your emergency patient through.'

'That should give us sufficient time to organise enough humidicribs,' Sally said briskly, and turned back into Pam's room, clearly believing that the decision had been made.

For several tense seconds David held Leah's gaze, almost as if he was finding it difficult to make a decision.

'Trust me,' Leah said softly, and for a moment it felt as if her heart was beating louder than the words. She hadn't realised just how much it mattered to her, and not just on a professional level.

He must have heard her because she saw the second when his tension eased and the single nod that followed.

'I'll see you in Theatre as soon as you can get there,' he agreed, and swung round to stride away again, then paused to look back over his shoulder. 'I do, you know,' he said cryptically.

'You do...what?' There was something almost fierce in his eyes now and it was scrambling her own logical thought processes so that she couldn't follow what he was talking about.

'I trust you,' he said seriously, and left her open-mouthed with surprise as she watched his long legs take him out of sight.

CHAPTER SIX

LEAH reversed her way through the doors, her scrubbed and gloved hands held carefully away from her body to prevent contamination.

'What's the score, Leah?' David demanded, and she was convinced that he must have eyes in the top of his head because she could swear that he hadn't looked up from his task.

She joined him on the opposite side of the table and saw that the patient was draped and ready for the word from the anaesthetist, her hand twined in a white-knuckled grip with her equally pale husband's.

She paused just long enough to give them both an encouraging smile before she answered David's question.

'There's no point trying terbutaline,' she said briefly. 'I left Sally getting her ready to come into Theatre.'

'Right.' He glanced up and met her eyes for a fraction of a second and when he didn't ask a single further question, she realised that he *did* trust her judgement.

'This is Rosalie Taylor,' he announced quietly, dragging her thoughts back from the quiet glow his confidence had given her.

'We know Dr Dawson,' Mike Taylor assured him in a voice made jerky by nerves. 'She's been monitoring Rosalie ever since the scan showed that the placenta was in the wrong place. We knew it was going to have to be a Caesarean birth because it was completely covering the cervix, but the baby isn't due for three weeks yet and then, suddenly, she went into labour and when she started to bleed…'

'It's all right, Mike,' Leah interrupted softly, understanding just how terrifying this must be for both of them. 'You got the three of you here safely before too much damage could be done. We're just waiting for the epidural to take effect, so all you need to do is make yourself comfortable so you're ready to give Rosalie the ringside commentary while we do our job. OK?'

He blew out a shaky breath then gave a nod and a strained smile. 'OK. One ringside commentary coming up.'

'Will I still be able to see the baby being born?' Rosalie asked anxiously, her glance going from Leah to David and back again. 'You did promise…'

David raised a dark eyebrow and those beautiful eyes spoke volumes without saying a word.

'As soon as we've done the gory bits,' Leah confirmed with a hint of challenge in her voice, hoping that David wouldn't object the way Donald had done. Her previous head of department hadn't liked anything to interfere with his work, but while she'd been running the department she'd discovered just how many of their new parents welcomed the opportunity to see their precious offspring's arrival, even though it couldn't be part of a normal delivery. 'If you still want to, we can drop the screen so you can see Baby Taylor's grand entrance into the world—*and* finally discover whether it's a boy or a girl!'

Even though half of his face was covered by a disposable mask, Leah saw a smile of approval light

David's eyes and welcomed the revelation that they were on the same wavelength on yet another topic.

'Just one word of caution,' he said to the parents-in-waiting, the serious tone completely at odds with his suddenly playful expression. 'Just because my face is the first one you see when the screen goes down, that doesn't mean you have to bond with me and take me home for the next eighteen years.'

'Ready when you are,' the anaesthetist announced over the startled burst of laughter, letting them know that the epidural had taken effect, and then there was no time for anything but concentrating on the mechanics of trying to deliver a healthy baby before the mother suffered serious blood loss.

'May I present the new Miss Taylor?' David announced just a few minutes later, as he lifted a squirming bundle out of the gaping incision and held her tenderly in both hands.

He'd long ago lost count of the number of times he'd performed this little ritual, but it never failed to lift his heart or bring a smile of satisfaction. It made all the years of study worthwhile when a risky delivery could be turned into a resounding success—especially one with such healthy lungs.

Without a word being spoken, Leah had clamped and cut the cord so that he could pass the squalling infant to Sally, and a moment later, wrapped in a warm blanket, their new daughter was placed in Rosalie's arms.

'Hello, precious,' she murmured, the words barely audible over the strident cries, then looked across at Leah. 'You wouldn't mind if we call her Leah, would you?' she asked. 'After all your help and understanding, we'd like to name her after you, but if you were saving that for your own daughter…'

If David hadn't been watching Leah's face he wouldn't have seen the flash of agony that crossed her face, but it was gone so fast, hidden behind smiling eyes, that he wondered if he'd imagined it.

Not that he had time to ponder the question, he thought as he concentrated on delivering the problematical placenta. He had to make certain that the cervix was undamaged if this young couple was going to be able to contemplate having more children without intervention. That didn't mean that his ears weren't listening for his pretty colleague's response.

'I would be honoured to have her named after me,' she said softly, sounding quite choked by the idea.

A quick glance in her direction told him that her soft grey eyes were glittering with the suspicion of tears and he was almost taken aback at the sight. Although he'd quickly realised that Leah cared deeply about all the aspects of the work she did, he'd had her pegged as too clinically involved with the processes to allow her emotions to become involved.

Those hastily hidden tears told another story completely. Inside the almost frighteningly efficient doctor who had not only managed to keep the department together but had also taken on extra duties such as conducting an overdue audit, there was a much softer person. And in spite of his determination to keep the rest of the world at bay, one bright glance from those grave grey eyes was enough to attract his attention, and when they gleamed with humour or sparkled with the threat of tears, it was all he could do to remind himself why he couldn't allow himself to weaken.

It wasn't until he was signing off on the paperwork

after the successful delivery of the Joliffes' twins and had to add the date that the most important of all those reasons was brought home to him full force.

'It's the seventeenth tomorrow,' he whispered around the sudden lump in his throat, the image of a laughing face and the memories of childish giggles searing his heart with the white heat of loss.

That was why he couldn't allow himself to weaken. There was no point in starting any sort of relationship with Leah, no matter how much he liked her as a doctor and a woman, because he couldn't bear to go through that sort of pain ever again.

In the meantime, there was the never-ending mountain of paperwork to climb...when he could fit it in between consultations, case reviews and the daily essentials of lab results. Sometimes it seemed as if the adrenaline-inducing trauma of an emergency Caesarean was the least stressful part of his day, especially when it resulted in healthy babies like the Joliffes' twins and little Leah Taylor.

Inside his head he carried the image of one Leah cradling the other and he was struck by a sudden painful desire to see her face soften at the sight of her own child...and his.

'*No!*' he exclaimed sharply, the agony in the single word echoing around his office just as her scrub-suited figure appeared in his open doorway.

He could have groaned aloud when he saw the way her ready smile disappeared.

'If you don't want to be disturbed, you should have shut your door,' she said crisply, and turned to stalk off.

'No!' he called again. 'Don't go, Leah. I wasn't talking to you.'

She paused just long enough to glare at him over her shoulder and her expression told him he would have to speak fast if he was to retrieve the situation. It wasn't her fault that his mood had been ruined by the realisation that it was the seventeenth tomorrow.

'I was having an argument with myself,' he said lamely, knowing that he couldn't tell her the real reason for his outburst. Perhaps his decision to run an open-door department needed a little refining. He'd believed that it would signal the fact that he was approachable, but if his private stresses were going to make him upset his staff...

He hadn't realised he was holding his breath until he saw her shoulders relax and a faint grin lift the corners of her mouth.

'Who won?' she teased, surprising an answering smile out of him.

That's when he knew he was in trouble, even though he didn't know how it had happened.

What was it about Leah that attracted him so much?

Granted, she was a beautiful woman, even in faded green scrubs. The crumpled baggy garb couldn't completely disguise her slender curves, and now it wasn't hidden under a disposable paper cap, her honey-coloured hair gleamed, but her heart-shaped face was dominated by the keen intelligence of those silvery grey eyes. She'd been all cool efficiency at first glance, but it hadn't taken long until he'd discovered the warmth and caring that were hidden just underneath.

But he'd known other women just as beautiful, just as intelligent and efficient and just as warm and caring. What was it about this particular combination that had started the revival of his long-dead emotions, the unwanted revival of emotions that he'd believed he'd buried for ever?

Whatever it was, it didn't matter. As the saying went, he'd been there, done that, seen the film, got the T-shirt and collected the broken heart. He couldn't go down that road again. It hurt too much.

Professional detachment...*that* was what he needed to concentrate on, not the fact that nothing more then the thought of Leah had his blood pumping faster, or the fact that the seventeenth was going to gut his emotions like a blunt knife.

'What on earth is the matter with the man?' Leah demanded in exasperation as she stripped off and climbed under the pelting spray of the shower at the end of a particularly gruelling afternoon.

It was a fact of life, working at the cutting edge of medical technology, that there were no guarantees, and today's disaster certainly proved it.

'I don't like it any better than he does,' she muttered, desperately trying to convince herself that the sting in her eyes was caused by her shampoo rather than the image of the tiny boy who hadn't stood a chance. 'Every time a baby dies it feels like a failure...for *all* of us.'

So why had David given her the silent treatment? He'd been glowering at her under dark brows as though it was *her* fault that India Smythe had lost her baby, but had that been nothing more than the final straw after a grim day?

Yesterday she'd thought that they were working really well together, especially when he'd let her know that he trusted her judgement over Pam Joliffe's treatment, but the last twenty-four hours had been dreadful.

'In fact, it's been going on ever since I caught him arguing with himself,' she mused, the urge to howl her eyes out diminishing as she remembered the welter of expressions that had crossed his face in a matter of moments.

She didn't think that it was a problem within the department, otherwise she was certain that he would have told her about it. He'd long since revised his initial impression that the department had descended into chaos with Donald's death. In fact, they'd even laughed together about the state of the office when he'd seen it in the final stages of her audit.

No, this was something else...something personal and private.

She grimaced, wondering if he was hiding a secret, too. Did he have a similar reason to her own as to why the department was such an all-important part of his life? There was certainly something putting that desolation in his eyes, even though he managed to keep it hidden most of the time.

'Whatever it is, it's none of your business unless it has an effect on the department,' she told herself firmly as she gave up on her determination to take the stairs to the top floor. After the day she'd had today, she really didn't need the exercise of climbing up to her flat, she rationalised as she watched the doors of the lift swish shut and the claustrophobic box lurched into action.

'And I'm definitely too tired to knock on his door and ask him what's been bugging him,' she muttered when the doors opened again, deliberately refusing to let her eyes stray towards that door.

She was just putting her key in the lock when she heard the sound of a thud and a crash just feet away from where she stood, closely followed by a very clear profanity.

Without another thought for what she could or should do, she was knocking sharply on the one door she'd been determined to avoid.

'David? Are you all right?' she demanded urgently. The visions of burglars attacking him that filled her head should have had her running in the opposite direction, but the possibility that he needed her help had her hammering on the unresponsive wood again. 'David! Do you need help?'

The sound of the lock being released made her step back a pace, suddenly aware that she couldn't be sure what she was going to be confronting.

A blood-spattered David ffrench was not one of the better scenarios she'd imagined, but it was exactly what was standing in the doorway.

That wasn't the only thing different about him either.

She'd grown so accustomed to seeing him in one of his smart suits when he was working at his desk or meeting patients for the first time that she actually managed to keep her eyes on her own work most of the time. His other persona, dressed in thin cotton scrubs that concealed nothing of his lean muscular body, was more difficult to ignore, especially when she was looking at him from the other side of the operating table and was treated to intimate glimpses of the pattern of dark hair that spread across his chest when he leaned forward.

This David ffrench, with rumpled hair and a bad-boy shadow on his chin and dressed in a paint-splattered polo shirt and a disreputable pair of jeans that were worn white in some very interesting places, was another person altogether.

Unfortunately, he was someone that made every one of her dormant hormones burst into life, no matter that any sort of relationship between them would be impossible, and the fact that her hands itched to touch that tousled hair and smooth it back from…the rivulets of blood trickling down his forehead?

'What on earth happened to you? Were you attacked?' she demanded, her heart inexplicably clenching in her chest at the thought that he was in pain. She peered uncertainly around his shoulders into the room beyond. Surely a burglar wouldn't just have allowed him to open the door like that.

'In a manner of speaking…if you count assault with a deadly picture frame,' he said with a pained chuckle, taking a crimson-streaked hand from a decidedly bloody head with a grimace. 'You might as well come in. I might need a hand to sort this mess out.'

As she reached for his arm, Leah's pulse was racing so hard it was making her feel quite light-headed.

'How badly have you damaged your hand?' she demanded, concerned for a moment about its effect on his professional life. Like many surgeons, he was adept with both hands, but to have the dexterity of one of them seriously impaired…

'Apart from a black nail where I hit it with the hammer, there's nothing wrong with my hand,' he said, leaning forward so that the top of his head was visible. 'All the blood's coming from my head.'

'Your head? How on earth did you manage that?' There was quite a gash hidden in the thick darkness of his hair and as was the usual case with head wounds, it was pouring blood in a steady stream.

'All too easily,' he said wryly as he led the way across his lounge. 'I'd been putting up a picture on the wall—the last of the unpacking in this room, thank goodness—but when I sat down to celebrate with a glass of wine while catching the news, the wretched thing fell down on my head.'

For a moment Leah had to fight the urge to chuckle at the image that painted, but then she saw him stoop to pick up some of the scattered glass.

'Hang on! Leave that till I've sorted your head out,' she ordered, grabbing for his arm. 'You'll be dripping gore all over the carpet and giving yourself another job to do. I presume you've got some sort of first-aid kit?'

He threw her an old-fashioned look and she couldn't help grinning.

'Well, you'd be surprised how many people don't,' she said. 'Now, let's get you to the bathroom and get you cleaned up.'

He muttered something indecipherable under his breath but did lead the way into the little room that was the mirror image of her own.

Except that hers felt bigger than David's, with plenty of room to move around, and there was the scent of a different brand of soap and shampoo in the air that made it seem as if the room was filled with his existence.

Her awareness of their proximity was made worse by the way she seemed to be bumping into him at every turn as he reached into the cupboard to take out a white tin with a prominent red cross on the top, then settled himself on the cork-topped stool beside the basin.

It was almost as if his presence sucked the oxygen

out of the room and she had to fight to stop her breathing growing shallow in response. And it was going to get worse.

'First of all, will you look at me so I can check your pupils?' she asked, hoping that he was more concerned with what she was seeing than in noticing her reaction to those beautiful blue-green eyes.

This close, the colour was even more stunning, reminding her of the changeability of light playing through water, and with those gold-tipped eyelashes and pupils large enough and dark enough to lose herself in their depths...

'Is there a problem?' he demanded, and she suddenly realised that she'd barely registered that both pupils were equal, neither had she checked that they were reactive to light. All she'd been doing had been gazing at them in admiration.

'No problem that I can see,' she reported briskly. 'It looks as if you escaped concussion, but if you start being sick or feeling nauseous—'

'I know the drill,' he interrupted, 'although how I'm supposed to be able to tell the difference between concussion-induced drowsiness and normal tiredness at the end of a hard week, I don't know.'

Glad that he didn't seem to have noticed her lapse in concentration, she busied herself with drawing some water in the basin then turned with one of his dark blue towels in her hands, knowing there was no way she was going to be able to put any distance between them while she tended his injury.

She wasn't going to allow herself to think about the fact that there was something...something magnetically attractive about the man that made her *want* to be close to him.

'If you lean your head over the edge of the basin, I'll be able to irrigate the cut and see just how bad it is.'

He perched the first-aid kit on one thigh, anchoring it there with his hand before resting his head on the towelling pad she'd fashioned to soften the edge of the white porcelain.

His hair was very thick and silky, with just enough natural curl to make it cling to her fingers as she sifted through it to expose his injury.

'It's bigger than I thought,' she said with a grimace. 'The edges are fairly clean but you should probably go into A and E for a couple of stitches if it's going to heal neatly.'

'I think I can trust you to do that for me,' he said as he straightened up far enough to show her just how well stocked his emergency kit was. Apart from the usual supplies, his contained several extras, including saline solution and sterile packs of swabs and needles, and while she was swiftly cataloguing them, he continued speaking. 'I'd rather not spend the rest of the evening waiting for attention while the staff deals with heart attacks and broken limbs. That's if you don't mind?'

Leah was glad he couldn't see the colour sweeping into her cheeks when he spoke of trust. It was just such a juvenile response for a woman already in her early thirties but she couldn't deny the warmth that spread through her.

'I can understand that you don't want to wait your turn for such a minor injury to be treated,' she murmured as she selected the things she'd need. 'Oh, dear. There's everything here except anaesthesia. It looks as if you're going to have to go in after all.'

'I've got a fairly high pain threshold, and it'll only be a couple of stitches,' he said stoically, and laid his head down again.

'It didn't sound like a high pain threshold from outside,' she pointed out, needing to keep up a distracting conversation—anything to steady the sudden tremor in her hand at the thought that she might hurt him. 'That was definitely more than a yelp I heard and the air in here was still distinctly blue around the edges when you opened the door.'

'Oops! Sorry about that, but it was the unexpectedness of having it land on my head like that,' he apologised, and she could have sworn that it was his turn to flush with embarrassment this time. 'I haven't been here long enough to find out how soundproof the walls are.'

'They're pretty good, unless someone's got the TV or stereo turned up loud,' she said as she trimmed the minimum amount of hair from either side of the gash so as not to leave the wound obvious after stitching. 'I just happened to be standing out on the landing at my door, or I probably wouldn't have heard a thing.'

'And I'd have been left here all on my own, bleeding to death,' he said in a pathetic little voice that had her chuckling at the whimsy of it even as she pierced his skin with the first suture.

She froze when she heard his sudden intake of breath.

'Are you sure about this?' she demanded, certain she could never allow anyone to do this to her without anything less than a full shot of local. 'We're only minutes away from A and E and I'm sure they would make an exception to the usual triage as you're a member of staff.'

'I'm OK. Let's just get it over with,' he said, but even though his voice was slightly muffled by his position, she was certain it sounded as if he was gritting his teeth.

Still, it was his body and his decision.

'Well, this is something we can never say to our patients when they're in labour, but…if you change your mind…!'

He gave a short huff of laughter then fell silent as she bent to her task again, determined to get it over with as quickly as possible for both their sakes.

'I washed the blood out of your hair so you don't need to get it wet again tonight, but it took three stitches to make a good job of it,' she announced as she straightened up a little later and began collecting the debris.

'I know. I was counting,' he said gruffly as he sent an exploratory hand up towards his head.

'Uh-uh! Don't touch!' She smacked his hand away. 'If you want to inspect my handiwork, I'll get a mirror.'

'Yes, Doctor. Thank you, Doctor,' he said, pretending meekness as he stood up to his full height.

She took a hasty step backwards, then another when he still seemed to be too close. Unfortunately, too many of her receptors were telling her brain that he wasn't nearly close enough.

'Can I make you a drink or would you like to join me in a glass of wine?' he offered. 'Luckily I only had white or I'd have made even more of a mess when I spilt it.'

Common sense told her it would be best for her peace of mind if she left straight away but when she opened her mouth to refuse, she found herself hesitating instead.

'Just a small glass,' he pressed persuasively as he led the way back into the lounge. 'I'm not having much myself after a knock on the head, but it does help the unwinding process before we go to bed.'

Before we go to bed?

Leah's brain stalled completely, filled not with thoughts of sharing a pleasant drink but with images of the two of them...naked...sharing his bed.

'Hang on a minute,' he said, and came to a halt so suddenly that she only just avoided ploughing right into his back. 'I've still got this mess to clear up. Would you like to pour the wine while I get rid of the glass?'

'Why don't you pour the wine while I do the clean-up?' she countered. 'You won't be very comfortable bending forward after you've had a knock on the head. It'll probably make it thump.'

They both reached for the picture that had caused all the problem, jostling for possession, and it was only when David's longer reach allowed him to swing it up from behind the chair that he revealed the other object that had been dislodged.

'No!' he exclaimed hoarsely, discarding the picture in his hand without a care for its survival as he stretched for the much smaller frame it had hidden. 'Oh, no!'

It almost sounded like despair in his voice and Leah felt a chill raise the hairs on her arms.

'What is it? Is it broken?' she asked as she angled her head to try to see what he was cradling so tenderly.

'Yes, it's shattered, and the glass has damaged the picture,' he added in a voice full of misery.

'What is it?' she repeated. 'Was it very valuable?'

There was desolation in his eyes when they finally met hers.

'It's precious, rather than valuable,' he said, and finally turned it around to show her a photograph of a chubby baby boy with an expression of absolute joy on his beaming face as he waved a brightly coloured toy at the camera. 'It's a photo of my…' He hesitated just long enough to draw in a jagged breath before he finished in a heart-breaking whisper. 'He was my son and he would have been one year old today.'

CHAPTER SEVEN

DAVID stifled a groan.

What on earth had possessed him to tell Leah about Simon?

That had been one of the reasons why he'd moved back to England—the fact that no one would know anything about his recent past.

Well, no one except his sister Maggie, and she was too deeply involved in her precious husband and equally precious new baby to do anything as crass as gossip about his failures.

Even Maggie knew nothing more than the bare bones of the facts. He hadn't been able to bring himself to admit to the sister who'd idolised him throughout their childhood that he'd been an utter fool, and the thought of baring his soul to a comparative stranger… Well, until a moment ago he would have said it was anathema.

Then he saw the empathy in Leah's soft grey eyes and knew why.

The two of them might not have been working together for very long, and she'd actually been antagonistic towards him at the beginning for being appointed to the post she'd wanted, but they'd soon overcome that with the discovery that they shared similar goals for the department.

Almost immediately, he'd realised that her professionalism was paramount, but over the time they'd been working together he'd also seen many examples of the way she related to their patients' feelings.

There were also the glimpses he'd had of the shadows that lurked behind her smiles, the hints that there had been tragedy in her life as well. Were these, too, the reasons why he'd known instinctively that Leah would understand?

And now she was looking at him with those big intelligent eyes and he knew that her sharp brain was busily cataloguing everything he'd said and matching it against his tone of voice and the expressions on his face.

He could only imagine what she'd seen when he'd caught sight of that precious photo lying in the shattered debris. The thought that it had been destroyed…that he had lost the last tangible proof that Simon had existed…

Emotion caught at his throat, making breathing difficult, and the hot press of tears threatened to overwhelm the stoic face he'd made a habit of showing to the rest of the world.

Afraid he was going to lose control and disgrace himself in front of her, he started to turn away but a single gentle hand on his arm stopped him in his tracks.

'Oh, David, I'm so sorry,' she murmured, and for the first time he felt as if someone wasn't just mouthing the usual social platitudes. Leah really meant the words because somehow she knew how much Simon had meant to him and how badly his loss had hurt.

After an almost totally trouble-free childhood—even he would have to admit that everything he'd attempted had come easily to him, whether it was sports or study—it had seemed that his adulthood was progressing the same way, with the job of his dreams and a beautiful wife and baby son.

From the first moment he'd known of the baby's existence, just weeks after he and Ann had met, he'd willingly planned a speedy marriage to legitimise his birth. Then, just weeks after his son was born, Ann had thrown the fact that he wasn't Simon's genetic father in his face.

He'd been devastated, but after the initial shock he'd discovered that it really hadn't mattered whose sperm had created the baby. Simon had been *his*.

Then Ann had taken Simon and just disappeared one day while he was at work, to go to join the man who'd fathered his precious son, and his bright plans for his future had died.

He'd built up so many pictures in his head of the things they'd do together as Simon grew older...helping him to walk and talk, ride a bike, play football...

'Even *that* I was able to rationalise,' he muttered, shocked to realise that the torrent of words hadn't just been running through his head but that he'd actually been voicing them to the slender woman sitting beside him on his settee, her grey eyes shimmering with sympathetic tears. 'I was able to tell myself that it didn't really matter who was his father as long as he had someone who would do all those things with him, but most of all who would love him...'

He bit his lip, but it didn't stop the first betraying tear sliding down his cheek. Suddenly he knew that nothing would stop the tears now. They had been dammed up for too long.

'But he didn't want him,' he forced out in a choked voice, feeling as if a vice was tightening around his chest. 'He didn't want my precious little boy and he sent Ann away... And she was driving when she shouldn't have been... And when the car came off the road...'

He couldn't go on, and then he didn't need to go on as Leah's arms slid around him to hold him close.

His last thread of restraint snapped and with a mixture of horror and utter relief he heard himself give in to the tears that felt as if they came direct from his heart.

'I'm...s-sorry,' he groaned into her shoulder, unable to stop the harsh sobs now that he'd started.

'Shh. It's not a problem,' she soothed, and he felt her hand begin to stroke him rhythmically—his back, his shoulder, his arm. 'Let it all out,' she whispered as she rocked him like a little child. 'Let all the poison out.'

And that was what it felt like, he realised with a distant sense of surprise. As he poured out his grief it was like the lancing of a hidden abscess that had been growing for month after month until there had been no room for anything else inside him.

He'd been doing his job and doing it well because that was all there was left for him. After the exposure of such a betrayal, followed so closely by the loss of his precious, loving child, he'd known that he would never be able to allow any woman close enough to hurt him again. The less a man had, he'd decided, the less he had to lose.

He'd just been lucky that when Maggie heard what had happened, she'd told him about the obs and gyn post being advertised at her hospital. With all his dreams shattered, he'd jumped at the chance to escape the wrenching memories to travel to the other side of the world again.

And he would probably have been able to keep working without the heartbreak overwhelming him— frantically busy for enough hours each day to ensure he was exhausted enough to sleep without dreams—if it hadn't been for the damage to the photo.

That precious image had been his lifeline back to the few blissfully happy memories of his disastrous marriage, the days when he'd revelled in the simple joys of fatherhood and believed that having Simon would be enough compensation for any amount of marital discord. To have lost that photo…

He lifted his head, uncomfortably aware that Leah must be regretting the day she'd ever met him. He was just so grateful that she had been there for him when the dam had burst, but what on earth must she be thinking about him for collapsing in such a way over nothing more than a photograph? Would he find one of the hospital's psychiatrists waiting to make an assessment of his mental competence when he arrived at work tomorrow?

But there was no condemnation in her eyes, not even a trace of discomfort that she'd seen him at his nadir. All he could see in those soft grey eyes was sympathy and acceptance and something more—understanding.

He'd guessed that there had been sadness in her life from the shadows he'd seen in her eyes and the special sensitivity she displayed when she dealt with patients who had spent years hopelessly longing to have a child.

For a fleeting moment he wondered if this was the right moment to ask her about the demons that lurked in her past, but then she lifted a hand to cup his cheek, her thumb gently stroking away the evidence of the last of his tears.

He would probably have felt nothing more than a lingering embarrassment at this evidence of his loss of control but then her gaze met his and, that quickly, the mood between them changed.

In the blink of an eye her protective embrace felt like something very different, her curves and hollows fitting him as though the two of them had been made to go together, and her soft mouth… Had he only just noticed how sweetly her lips curved? He couldn't imagine waiting another moment to know if her mouth was as soft and as sweet as it looked.

And it was, every bit as soft and sweet, but it was also hotter than he could have imagined and more inviting, and when she welcomed him inside, he found the one place in the world where all the pain and misery couldn't follow.

Between one breath and the next they were wrapped in each other's arms, not one offering comfort while the other accepted but both giving and receiving pleasure equally while desire rose to twine about them.

'Leah! Oh, Leah!' he groaned when their naked bodies met for the first time. Without a word being spoken they had each known instinctively what the other had wanted and the best way to achieve it, their minds and bodies every bit as closely attuned in their passion as they were in the operating theatre.

But this was no clinical procedure. This was two eager bodies cleaving together in a maelstrom of emotions, need and compassion and desire and acceptance and even absolution.

At the last moment, with his last shred of sanity, he paused long enough to demand, 'Are you protected?'

'What?' she panted, dragging her gaze up from the point where his body had been about to disappear inside hers.

Her pupils were huge and dark with arousal and he nearly ignored the warning voice inside his head, but the memories of Simon were too close and too painful. He wouldn't risk going through any of that again.

'I'm clean—I haven't been with anybody for more than a year—but I haven't got anything with me and I don't want to get you pregnant,' he said gruffly. 'Are you protected?'

A spasm of despair crossed her face but her voice only wavered slightly when she answered.

'You don't have to worry,' she whispered, but her pain was as clear to him as if she'd shouted, and he suddenly knew what was coming. 'I can't have children.'

He closed his eyes and when he pressed his forehead to hers he could feel the quiver of tension that thrummed through her, could feel her pain.

'I'm sorry,' he said, even as he knew how inadequate the words were. At least he'd had Simon for a little while, whereas Leah… No wonder she could empathise with the women they treated. She'd obviously walked at least a mile in their shoes.

He lifted his head and forced himself to meet her gaze, every nerve screaming with the knowledge that in his caution he'd probably ruined any chance of ever making love with this beautiful, complex, loving woman, but he was honour-bound to give her the choice, even though they had come this close.

'Leah, would you rather not…?'

He heard her draw in a sharp breath and as her

mouth tightened into a narrow line he saw the spark of indignation in her eyes.

'Don't you find me attractive enough to desire me now you know I'm a barren woman?' she demanded, and he laughed aloud. Surely she knew how ridiculous that was? Didn't she look in a mirror?

'Not find you attractive?' He directed her gaze down their bodies, his own still blatantly poised to take full advantage of her body's silent invitation. He deliberately ignored the little voice in a tiny corner of his mind. The fact that she was the first woman since Ann's betrayal to have any effect on his hormones was perfect since her inability to have a child probably made her the ideal woman for him. 'You must be joking!'

'That's just biology,' she said dismissively. 'It doesn't mean that it's *me* that you—'

He cut her off by the quickest and easiest route, his mouth stopping her lips and tongue from voicing any more words, then persuading them to speak another language entirely.

Long seconds later he lifted his head again, pleased to see she was every bit as short of breath as he was.

'In case you didn't get the message, let me say it in words of one syllable,' he growled, teasing both of them by brushing his body lightly over hers and having the satisfaction of feeling her instinctively arch up in response to deepen the contact. 'It's never happened to me like this before, and I don't know what sorcery you've used to make it happen now but, *yes*, I want you. Here and now, I want you. Any way I can have you, I want you. Now, please, woman, will you put me out of my agony?'

It took a second for his words to register but the

smile that bloomed across her face warmed him right to his bones, and then she raised a single quizzical eyebrow.

'Put you out of your *agony*?' she questioned with a hint of bravado in her voice as she deliberately wrapped first one slender leg and then the other around his hips. 'You don't know what agony is...*yet*!' she promised as she tightened her grip and drew him into the hot dark depths of her body for the first time.

For a moment Leah lay with her eyes closed, wondering why she felt so exhausted, then she felt the heavy weight of David's possessive arm around her waist and she *knew* why.

Her face heated with the memory of how brazen she'd been during the night, taunting him into that first blazing inferno on his settee then inviting him to join her in the bathroom for the most sensual bubble bath of her life...or had that been *after* he'd carried her to his bed and made slow delicious love to her until she'd barely been able to breathe, let alone even the score?

Her brain was on emotional overload, whirling with so many images from the hours they'd spent together that it was almost impossible to single one out from the rest. But that didn't stop her logic from posing the important question—where did they go from here?

Last night had been something special, she admitted silently, and that wasn't just the starry-eyed opinion of an innocent. She'd been married and had known the early days of excitement and experimentation. She'd also charted their decline into desperation and disillusionment when she and Gordon had been trying to have a baby. But even at its best, it had been nothing like this and she didn't know why.

Was it the novelty of a different partner? After all, Gordon had been the first and only man she'd slept with until last night. Or had it been the element of catharsis that had made everything seem so much *more* than it had ever been before? More exciting, more erotic, more tender, more intimate, but most of all more fulfilling.

Or had it been the fact that, until David had let her inside his protective shell and shown her his wounded soul, she hadn't been able to admit to herself that she'd been slowly falling in love with him from the first time he'd looked at her with those beautiful but wary blue-green eyes?

Where did they go from here, now that the night was over?

What would happen when he woke up this morning?

Logic told her that he was unlikely to declare his undying love for her as soon as he opened his eyes. If he'd been going to do that, there had been plenty of opportunities during the night, and he hadn't taken one of them.

Would he actually resent the fact that she was still in his bed, an unwelcome reminder of the fact that she'd been a witness to the moment when he'd lost his tight control on his emotions?

With a feeling akin to dread she silently acknowledged that a night that had been nothing less than a magical revelation for her could turn out to be a disaster where their working relationship was concerned. And they'd been working so well together, sharing the burdens of running a busy department with more than the average levels of stress as seamlessly as if they'd been colleagues for years.

Panic began to flood through her as she imagined

how difficult it would be to do something as simple as share their office if there was a barrier of embarrassment between them, and as for the strained atmosphere when they shared an operating theatre, with patients' lives and happiness in their hands... It didn't bear thinking about.

So, what was she going to do about it?

She didn't have enough experience to be able to carry off a blasé morning-after-the-night-before scene with any degree of believability, and without knowing what he felt about their time together she could hardly wait around expecting some hearts-and-flowers scene where they fell into each other's arms and vowed eternal fidelity.

No, by far the best answer was to leave as quickly and as quietly as she could, before he had a chance to wake, and keep her fingers crossed that the first time they met each other today would be in the middle of a throng of other people. Once that first meeting was over, she would know just how much damage their encounter had done to their working relationship and would have to decide what she was going to do about it.

As for the damage to her heart, that was another matter and something she definitely didn't have time to think about yet.

David silently berated himself for a coward as Leah slid surreptitiously out of his bed.

For a moment he was tempted to tighten his arm around her, suddenly struck by a ridiculous fear that he was about to let something infinitely precious out of his grasp, but he resisted the urge.

Hoping that she wouldn't realise that he was already

awake, he kept his eyes closed but he didn't need to be able to see her setting off in search of her scattered clothing to imagine how perfect her slender body would look in the subdued light of his bedroom clothed only in that lustrous fall of honey-blonde hair. He'd spent hours admiring it during the night, and exploring it and enjoying every sweet, giving, enticing, welcoming inch. In fact, he didn't know how he was going to be able to meet those soft grey eyes again without picturing her in all her naked glory.

And that was going to be a problem.

Thus far he'd had no trouble treating her as just another colleague, even when the scent of her shampoo wreathed its way around their office. The heartbreak he'd been through had armoured him against even the most attractive of women…until she'd appeared on his doorstep last night just as he'd reached the limits of his endurance.

The soft click of his front door closing sounded as clearly as a rifle shot through the silent flat, and he bolted to his feet.

'What a stupid thing to have done!' he snarled as he began to pace, uncaring that he was still stark naked. 'At the very least you could have ruined a very satisfactory working relationship, and at the worst…' For a moment he couldn't decide whether it would be more of a disaster to be hauled over the coals for sexual harassment of a female junior member of staff or if that member of staff should take it into her head that she'd fallen madly in love with him and expect an ongoing relationship.

'Any of those would be a disaster!' he groaned as he set off for the bathroom then groaned a second time when he realised he was never going to be able to enter the room again without seeing Leah in there with him…surrounded by bubbles in the bath, or with her curves outlined by rivulets of water under the shower, or with her face halfway between agony and ecstasy as he lifted her onto the edge of the vanity unit and buried himself in her depths.

'Mrs Thompson…Julia…I can't tell you how sorry I am, but as you've seen on the ultrasound, the baby's heart isn't beating any more,' David said to their sobbing patient, and just from the rough edge to his voice, Leah knew he meant every word.

It was the first time she'd seen him since she'd slipped out of his bed that morning but there was no time to even think about their personal lives. They were facing a situation that, out of all the scenarios she came across in her work, was guaranteed to put a dark cloud over the department—a full-term baby that, for some inexplicable reason, had simply died before the mother had gone into labour.

It was bad enough when patients lost their precious babies in the first few weeks of gestation, but to have come so close to success…to have spent all those weeks and months nurturing and loving and anticipating, only to have it snatched away without warning…

'So, what happens now?' asked an ashen-faced Trevor Thompson. 'Do you have to operate to…?' He couldn't finish.

'A Caesarean is major surgery, with all the risks that entails, and because it also permanently damages the uterus, we only use it if the life of the mother or the baby is at risk.'

This was another important point on which she and David were in complete agreement—that their department would not condone the use of surgery just for convenience. Much to the disgust of some staff and patients who wanted to avoid the uncertain timetable of natural birth, it was now only used as a last resort. Those who wanted Caesareans on demand to suit their social lives now had to pay to go elsewhere.

'In a little while we'll be putting up a drip to induce labour,' he went on gently. 'Sally, your midwife, will explain it all to you and give you the option of having an epidural to make things less painful.'

'*Nothing* could make it less painful!' Julie said vehemently, losing her fight with the next flood of tears. 'I'm going to have to go all the way through labour *knowing* that my baby's d-dead! I'm never going to be able to h-hold it or—'

'Of course you can hold your baby!' Leah exclaimed, her own eyes stinging with the threat of tears. 'You'll finally find out if it's a girl or a boy and you'll name it and spend time with it…as much time as you need so you can start to grieve for what you've lost.'

'But I thought…' Trevor shrugged. 'I remember something about babies being taken away before the mothers saw them.'

'Unfortunately, that used to happen a lot in the mistaken belief that if it was out of sight it was out of mind,' Sally admitted. 'Some mothers went the whole of their lives convinced that their babies hadn't died at all but had been stolen and were still alive somewhere. Once we realised what a dreadful effect it could have on the mother's mental well-being, we made certain that we changed our policies. Now it's very much centred on what the *parents* want. I can promise you that you won't be rushed into anything, and if either of you want to speak to someone—a counsellor, a priest, your parents or even one of us—all you have to do is ask.'

For some reason Leah was reluctant to leave the room, but unless there were unexpected complications, she wasn't needed any more. Sally was very good at her job and had obviously formed a good relationship with the couple during their antenatal visits. Leah had confidence that the experienced midwife would do everything she could to make such an awful event a little more bearable.

'What is the protocol here?' David asked quietly as they walked back towards the office, all awkwardness over their night together apparently pushed to one side by the sadness of more recent events. 'Does Sally inform the coroner once the baby's born or do we? And how long does it take to get the results of post-mortem examinations?'

She gave him the information by rote, wondering if he was waiting until they reached the privacy of their shared space before he said anything, but almost as soon as they entered the room the phone rang.

From then on it seemed as if there was hardly time to breathe before they were hurrying towards Theatre to start a busy list.

The first patient, undergoing her first cycle of IVF, should have been gently relaxed by her pre-meds, but the adrenaline of knowing that they were going to be harvesting her eggs today still had her bouncing off the walls with a mixture of fear and excitement.

'I don't need to ask if you want Peter to come in with you,' Leah teased gently, gesturing towards their tightly entwined hands. Her husband was already decked out in scrubs and looking rather self-conscious but with a determined air about him.

'Well, I'm going to be out for the count so I need him to keep score while you're collecting them,' Carol Stanford said. 'My grandmother used to keep chickens, and when I stayed with her I used to collect the eggs. If I managed to find more than a dozen, she used to scramble the extra ones and we had them for breakfast on a piece of toast.'

'Well, I'm not sure whether you'll need much toast for these eggs,' Leah warned as she gave Ashraf a nod to commence anaesthesia. 'They *are* going to be rather small.'

'I don't mind how small they are…just as long as there's…lots…' She only just managed to finish the sentence before the anaesthetic claimed her.

'Ready, Peter?' Leah invited as she kicked the lock off the trolley wheels and helped to aim it towards the theatre. 'One of the nurses will give you a stool to sit on by Carol's head. You'll be able to hold her hand while you're watching the screen to keep an eye on what we're doing.'

Once in the theatre, professionalism took over as she and David manipulated the microscopic camera through the neat incision to examine the swollen ovaries and then, one by one, aspirated each egg that had been triggered into ripening by the cocktail of hormones.

It was delicate and time-consuming work, especially at the start of the procedure. Sometimes weeks of nasal sprays and painful injections only resulted in three or four eggs, but as today's tally mounted, the atmosphere in the room became almost giddy with relief at their success.

By the time Stanley had checked the count under

the microscope in the lab, Carol was in Recovery and already surfacing from the anaesthetic.

'Hello, Carol…Peter. How are you doing?' Leah greeted them, one hand hidden behind her back.

'Great!' Carol said. 'Groggy but great! Peter said there were lots of eggs but he didn't know how many.'

'What *was* the final count when you got them to the lab?' Peter demanded eagerly. 'Was it more than six in the end?'

'Six babies!' Carol exclaimed euphorically before Leah could answer, and she hurried to caution both of them in case they had unrealistic expectations. She knew only too well that there were absolutely no guarantees with IVF.

'Remember what we said about not counting your chickens?' she warned. 'There's no guarantee that they'll all fertilise successfully, or that they'll go on to develop properly for implantation. And even if they *are* successfully implanted, there's still only an average of—'

'A one in five chance of success,' they chorused, the statistics clearly doing nothing to dampen their elation at having got this far.

'We know all that,' Peter reassured her more soberly, then his eyes brightened. 'But just for a little while it's nice to terrify ourselves with the prospect of every one of those eggs becoming a real live baby. So, tell us. How many did you harvest in the end?'

'Does this give you a clue, Carol?' Leah said with a broad grin as she took the plate of toast out from its hiding place behind her. 'Didn't your grandmother give you toast for the extra eggs if you collected more than a dozen?'

CHAPTER EIGHT

IF LEAH had thought that there would be time to talk at the end of their list, she'd been wrong.

That evening, she'd sat at her desk in their shared office for several hours battling with a pile of post-operative paperwork and then completed a mountain of routine form-filling with her ears straining for the familiar sound of David's footsteps coming towards her along the corridor. To boost her courage she was freshly showered and had donned the smart trousers and shirt she kept as a standby in her locker. She knew that outwardly she looked cool and professional, but inside her heart was still beating so fast she could almost hear the sound echoing off the freshly painted walls...but he'd never arrived.

At first, she'd put the fact that she hardly saw him, let alone spoke to him, down to coincidence. It had actually taken several days of missed opportunities before the penny had dropped and she'd realised that he must be deliberately avoiding her.

'Well, that tells me how much that night meant to him!' she'd muttered as he'd disappeared around the corner yet again, murmuring something almost incomprehensible about a meeting he needed to attend, leaving her feeling a complete fool.

It was bad enough that, in spite of all her determination, she'd fallen in love with the man. She'd quickly discovered that it was even worse to have him treating her as if she were carrying a plague.

Had he guessed at her feelings? Had she somehow given herself away? Or was it just that she'd become so besotted with the man that she'd simply misunderstood his motives? Perhaps he hadn't seen that precious night as anything more than a single night of comfort…a time out of time to take his mind off the fact that it should have been Simon's first birthday? With the brutal honesty of hindsight, she realised that she didn't really know what he'd wanted from her. Perhaps he was even afraid that she might try to trap him into a more permanent relationship.

Was that why he seemed to be afraid of spending any time with her? Did he think that she was going to grab him and demand a wedding ring if he spent a single minute in her company that wasn't strictly work-orientated?

'Well, I've got two choices,' she announced to the empty room, glad that she'd closed the door to signal that she wanted to be left undisturbed for a while. She really didn't want to have her private conversations with herself broadcast right through the department. It was bad enough that they happened in the first place.

'I can either confront the man—and risk making the atmosphere between us even worse—or I can just ignore him the way he's ignoring me and continue to give all my attention to the job.'

Neither option made her very happy.

The two of them had been working so well together right up until that night, the workload seeming far less onerous when they were tackling it together.

Still, in spite of the fact that it had made her working life less pleasant, she had to admit that there was no way she would have missed the magic of that night. It had given her memories that would last for ever and had been worth every bit of the continuing tension between them.

It was up to her to get over her longing for more of the same. Obviously David didn't feel the same way.

This was killing him, David thought as the scent of Leah's soap reached him from her position just inches away—or was it her shampoo? In spite of the hours they'd spent in each other's arms he hadn't been able to work it out, not when the underlying scent of warm woman had been enticing him to madness. And now that he was trying to put a bit of distance between the two of them, he couldn't even make an excuse to ask.

Anyway, he needed to concentrate on something, *anything* but the scent of Leah's body. He was supposed to be working. He had a worried couple sitting on the settee in front of him who had been waiting for the results of the last lot of tests they'd had done. After all their years of heartbreak, the Whittiers wouldn't appreciate the fact that his mind wasn't on his work because all he could think about was what he'd rather be doing...

He cleared his throat and had to shuffle the sheaf of papers on his lap to hide his body's all too obvious reaction to his thoughts, wondering for a mad moment why he didn't just change his mind and mix a little pleasure into their business relationship.

It would be such a blissful relief from unremitting nights of misery if he could just sink into the welcoming depths of her body, and if he was reading Leah's eyes in her unguarded moments, it wouldn't take much persuasion for her to agree to a repeat performance.

One part of his brain was following the conversation as Leah did her best to put the anxious couple at their ease, but the other part was trying to talk some sense into himself.

Yes, he would welcome the chance to burn up the sheets again with Leah, but even though it would ease his immediate obsession with her it wouldn't be fair to either of them. In spite of his attraction to her, he certainly didn't want any sort of permanent relationship, not after his disastrous attempt with Ann. And, anyway, unless his instincts were off the mark, Leah wasn't the sort of woman to settle for an affair and that was all he could offer.

The bit of office gossip he'd picked up since he'd come to St Luke's had confirmed that her colleagues knew virtually nothing about her private life—just the fact that she didn't date anyone from the hospital. He wouldn't allow himself to think about why that thought pleased him.

His own observations of the long hours she spent in the department had told him that she had time for little besides her work. One of the younger midwives had even hinted that she might be a lesbian and he'd nearly laughed in her face. He knew only too well that Leah was definitely heterosexual...a fact that was replayed in graphic detail every night whether he was awake or dreaming.

She'd revelled in everything they'd done together, quickly getting over her initial reticence to be the most sensual lover he'd ever had... And here she was, perfectly poised and so very professional in her charcoal-grey pinstripe trouser suit with not a honey hair out of place—unlike that night when it had been spread across his pillow or draped over his naked body or...

Suddenly he realised that all three of the other people in the room were throwing him some strange glances and with a flash of horror for whatever his unguarded expression might have revealed, he had to force his thoughts back to the meeting in progress.

What on earth was the matter with him?

He'd never had a problem with his thoughts wandering like this before. He wouldn't have risen so far, so fast in his profession if he hadn't been able to keep his mind on what he was doing. What had happened to his concentration?

As it was, he'd barely noticed that Leah had started going through the results of the battery of tests the couple had undergone, from the blood test on the woman to determine whether she was ovulating to the swim test on the man's sperm to confirm their number and whether they had sufficient motility to reach their goal once they'd been released.

'So,' she was summarising with another uneasy glance in his direction, before she returned to the anxious husband, 'we now know that there's nothing wrong with your sperm. It has the same proportion of non-swimmers and swimmers with absolutely no sense of direction as the majority of the male population, and also the same proportion of really determined ones that know exactly where they're going and why.' She turned to the wife next. 'And we now know that there's nothing wrong with your system either. All your plumbing is in normal working order and you're ovulating regularly, too. We've also established that there's no chemical incompatibility between the two of you that prevents conception.'

'So, you're saying that everything's working properly?' James Whittier summarised with an entirely male expression of relief on his face that their problems weren't his 'fault'.

'Exactly,' Leah said.

'But I'm still not getting pregnant, so…where do we go from here?' demanded Sonia, obviously frustrated by the ultimate lack of answers after all the weeks of poking and prying and waiting. 'Can we have IVF?'

'Before we make that decision, we'd like you to have a meeting or two with one of our staff psychologists,' David interrupted, even though he knew Leah didn't really need him jumping in. She'd been successfully conducting these interviews for months before he'd been appointed, but he had a feeling that the only way for him to keep his mind on the right track was to actually take part in the conversation.

'A psychologist!' James exclaimed, clearly disgusted by the suggestion. 'Don't tell me you think it's all in our minds! What's he going to do—hypnotise us into getting pregnant?'

'You'd be surprised the lengths that some couples will go in their attempts to have a baby,' David said in a calming voice. 'Changing their diets to cut out all junk food, aromatherapy, Australian bush flower sheoak essence, changing their underwear if they wear thongs…all sorts of things. And you'd also be amazed at how successful some of them are—but that's not why we want you to go.' He leaned forward to add weight to his words.

'The two of you already know just how frustrating and stressful it's been while you've been going through all the various tests,' he continued, waiting just long enough for them to nod their agreement before he went on. 'We want you to have a word with the psychologist because she'll be taking you through the implications of embarking on an IVF programme.'

'I hope the implications are that we'll end up with a baby,' James interrupted gruffly.

'We hope so,' David agreed evenly. 'It would be wonderful if you were one of the one in four couples who are successful, but there are also risks beyond the physical stresses on Sonia that you'll need to consider.'

'Such as?' his petite wife prompted with a frown.

'Such as the fact that IVF is a long hard road without any guarantee of success, and that there's a definite possibility that having to undergo repeated unsuccessful cycles could have serious effects on your marriage.'

'But if it's our only option…' James said, his tone a cross between belligerence and despair.

'There's also adoption,' Leah suggested gently. 'Have you considered that?'

'Not until we've tried all the other options,' James said firmly. 'If there's a possibility that we can have our own child—one that's a part of each of us—then we'd rather do that first. For me, adoption would be much further down the road. A last resort, if everything else had failed.'

'That's a decision for the two of you to make, of course, but first give yourselves a little time to come to terms with what you've found out today.'

'No!' Sonia exclaimed urgently. 'I want to make the appointment straight away.' Her pale blue eyes flicked from Leah to David and back again as though fearful that they might try to stop her putting her argument. 'Every day that goes by I'm getting older and my chances of getting pregnant go down and the chance of IVF working gets less. I don't want to waste any more time, especially if it takes several cycles before I get pregnant. We want to be young enough to be able to do all the usual things with our child that other parents do. It wouldn't be any fun for him or her if the two of us need Zimmer frames just to go the park to feed the ducks.'

David joined in the laughter then joined in the farewells as Leah escorted the couple out to organise their first appointment with the psychologist. He nearly groaned aloud when he realised that his eyes were greedily following every gentle sway of Leah's slender hips as she walked away.

'When am I going to be able to forget what she looks like under those smart business clothes?' he growled, but if he was honest, he already knew the answer. Never.

Leah buried her face in her hands and sighed heavily.

It seemed impossible that everything had changed so much in the last month or so.

She thought back to the morning she'd learnt of David ffrench's imminent arrival and her sharp disappointment that he was to take up the position as AR department head that she'd set her heart on. She'd be less than honest if she didn't admit that it had been a blow to her ego and a setback to her ambitions. It would also be dishonest if she didn't admit that the longer she'd worked with David, the more she appreciated his clinical skills and his surgical ability. And as for the man himself...

The heat that seeped through her with nothing more than a passing thought about him said more than enough about the way she felt about him, and that was in spite of the fact that he'd turned into a taciturn porcupine since that night they'd spent together. Well, it wasn't his fault that he hadn't fallen in love with her, too, and if his avoidance tactics were the result of embarrassment that he'd let his guard down on the anniversary of his son's birthday, she could soon put his mind at rest if only he'd give her a couple of minutes to speak to him in private. It would only take that long to promise him that she'd keep his confidences to herself.

Her intermittent lack of concentration was bad enough, but the air of misery that had descended over the department during the last week or so was something else entirely.

'I bet I know what you're thinking about,' said Sally's voice from the doorway. 'You've got the same expression on your face as David.'

Leah hoped her expression hadn't also betrayed the sudden leap her pulse had taken at his name, but she beckoned the midwife in, smiling her thanks for the second mug of coffee she'd brought with her.

'It was bad enough when one of the Masson triplets went down with necrotising enterocolitis,' Leah said grimly before trying to take a sip of liquid that was still far too hot to drink.

'Well, he was the smallest and weakest but until then he'd seemed to be managing to hold his own,' Sally agreed, perching her own mug on the corner of the desk and peering into a paper bag that rustled enticingly. 'The onset was so insidious that we'd only just worked out what was wrong with him, so when it suddenly flared out of control...' The progression to generalised sepsis had been so virulent that there had been little anyone could do, and within hours he'd been dead.

'Then there was the shoulder dystocia,' Leah continued, feeling sick all over again as she remembered the moment during that delivery when she'd thought they were going to lose that baby, too. At the last moment one twin had interfered with the safe delivery of the other, and in trying to deliver both without risking oxygen starvation and brain damage, one had ended up with a broken clavicle.

She put her coffee aside untasted, suddenly finding the smell of it too rich.

'At least it turned out reasonably well in the end. Both babies arrived with good Apgar scores, but Mum isn't at all happy with the size of her episiotomy or the number of stitches you had to put in,' Sally said with a grimace.

They both knew that an abnormally large cut was unavoidable with some of the complications of malpresentation, but they could hardly ask a woman in pain whether she would rather her babies had been put at risk for the sake of fewer stitches.

'And that's just down at your end of the department,' Leah said. 'You'll have heard about the run of heartbreak cases up at this end, too. The last few days we've had more than our share of patients with diagnoses that…well, with the best will in the world, all we could do was tell them that there was nothing we could do for them.'

They were the cases that Leah thought about in the middle of the night, wondering how the couples were coming to terms with the verdict that they would never be able to conceive and carry the baby they longed for. Some were stunned into silence by the conclusion while others were furious, convinced that the mediahyped miracle of IVF was being unfairly withheld from them.

'Then we've had several patients who only managed

to produce four or five eggs to harvest after all those weeks of hormone therapy, and a higher than usual failure rate for implantations,' Leah finished, completing the litany of disasters.

'So, what do you think we should do to perk everyone up?' Sally demanded, silently offering to share the second half of her onion-laden hot dog with Leah. 'It can't be good for the department to have everyone going around with long faces. We'll be frightening all the customers away.'

Leah shook her head at the offered food, her stomach turning over queasily at the greasiness of it, but before she could make any suggestions about raising department morale, Sally's pager shrilled.

'Cross your fingers that this is going to be a delivery that goes as easily as shelling peas,' she said, then stuffed the last of the hot dog into her mouth in one huge bite even as she was snagging her coffee and making for the door.

Was that all it was? Leah wondered. Was it just a run of sad cases that had her feeling so down and out of sorts, or was it more than that? Was it also because she was angry that David's change of attitude towards her had robbed her of part of her enjoyment of her job?

There had always been patients they couldn't help and, given the nature of the work they did, there would always be more failures per IVF cycle than there were successes. Even those successes weren't immune to the occasional tragedy during labour, but the birth of each normal, healthy baby was a comforting reward for all their efforts.

She wasn't just fascinated by the mechanics of monitoring hormone levels, harvesting eggs, fertilising them and then returning them to the mother's body, hopefully to have them implant and develop normally for an uneventful nine months. She also took great satisfaction from the intellectual side—the puzzle-solving involved as they tried to identify and isolate the reasons why each individual patient wasn't able to conceive the baby they so desperately wanted or maintain a pregnancy for a viable length of time.

Once they'd overcome their initial wariness of each other, she'd enjoyed sharing her philosophy with David and had felt a growing bond with him when she'd discovered how many goals they shared—a bond that had apparently been severed for ever by that night.

Determined to break the interminable circular track of her thoughts, she reached for the mug of rapidly cooling coffee, but before the liquid even touched her lips, nausea rose up in her throat and cold perspiration covered her body.

On shaky legs she took the mug across to the basin and tipped it out. Holding her breath, she rinsed every trace of it away then abolished even a hint of the smell with a swish of the antiseptic tea-tree soap the department used on their hands to help prevent the spread of infection.

'So…' she whispered when she sat down again, still feeling sick and out of sorts but with a quiver of something electric, too. 'What's *this* all about? I haven't heard anything about a bug doing the rounds, so is this just an emotional reaction because I'm angry with David for building that wall, or because…?'

She couldn't even give voice to the possibility that she was pregnant. The whole idea was impossible…unthinkable.

It had taken so long for her to get even that far when

she'd been married. Month after month she'd cried when her body had produced the bright evidence that once more she'd failed to conceive. Surely fate wouldn't be so cruel as to make it happen so easily as the result of a one-night stand.

Her eyes were burning with the threat of tears when she'd thought she had none left. She'd cried a whole lifetime's supply of them in the years when she'd been married to Gordon, her hopes alternately raised and then dashed by each failure.

Knowing how much it had hurt her in the past— how close the failure had come to destroying her—she had sworn that she wouldn't ever go through it again. But here she was—one second her heart soaring as she imagined the tiny fragile beginnings of a new life deep inside her and the next plummeting to earth, knowing that even if she *had* conceived, the child would never live long enough for her to hold it in her arms.

She scrubbed her hands over her face and straightened her shoulders, drawing in a deep breath to steady the nerves still quivering in her stomach.

'There's one sure way to put my mind at ease,' she muttered, getting to her feet with a return to her usual determination. 'I'll send a sample up to the lab. Stanley will soon let me know that it's all in my imagination.' And then she could start coming to terms with yet another hope dashed. She already knew that it was futile to wish that it could actually be true—that she really *was* pregnant with David's child and that this time she would actually be able to carry it to term.

David allowed himself a silent sigh of relief that he had the office to himself for a few minutes, then found himself unable to make a start on the everlasting paperwork.

Even though he reminded himself at intervals that it was none of his business, he was worried about Leah.

When he'd first arrived at St Luke's, she'd been a live wire with enough energy and determination for at least three grown men.

'Talk about multi-tasking!' he muttered. For heaven's sake, she'd been doing her own job and Donald's as well...and she'd *still* found time to conduct a major audit and redecorate the office.

She certainly didn't seem to be the same person any more. Oh, she was still brilliant at her job, but she was so quiet and self-effacing these days, almost as though she didn't want him to notice she was there.

It was killing him by inches!

For a start, he wasn't sleeping worth a damn, and when he did finally drop off, his dreams were every bit as hot as his memories of that night, and left him wanting more, too.

As for work... He groaned aloud and rammed his fingers through his hair, knowing that the problems they were having were all of his own making. He'd been so worried that she might get the wrong idea about his intentions after they'd spent the night together that he'd completely stonewalled her, and now he was reaping the results. She barely spoke to him any more, and that couldn't continue. In such a busy department, there were things about which he desperately needed her input.

Last night, he'd actually started thinking about his options. He'd even got as far as thinking about moving house or changing jobs before he had some sort of a breakdown, until he realised how ridiculous he was being. He didn't want to change his job, and, even though it was playing havoc with his sleep patterns and the fit of his trousers, he didn't want to move away from Leah.

In the meantime, there was a paper he'd been asked to present at an IVF symposium—if he ever got any time to prepare it—and an interminable Mount Everest of paperwork to do.

'Why are there never enough hours in the day?' he growled in frustration, and picked up the latest batch of test results. He'd been toying with some ideas for streamlining the system and now that he needed another informed point of view as to whether they were workable, it wasn't available. Leah was the obvious person to ask—the one person in the department who would understand what he was trying to achieve and whose opinion he would trust to be logical and unbiased—and he'd totally alienated her.

Well, that situation couldn't go on or the department would start to suffer. Something was going to have to change and it was up to him to change it, even if he had to make a grovelling apology for his inappropriate behaviour.

Surprised that his burden seemed to have lightened fractionally just by the fact that he'd decided to take action, he reached for the first set of test results back from the lab and tried to access the patient's file on the computer.

'Not found? Check spelling and reference number,' he groaned aloud as the message appeared on the screen. 'How many ways can you spell Jane Smith, for heaven's sake?'

Impatiently, he tried again, with the same result.

With a frown, he read the brief details on the result sheet and realised that he didn't recognise the patient. Had the result been sent to the wrong department? That was unlikely, knowing what a tight ship Stanley ran.

'Anyway, it was a check for the level of pregnancy hormones, so that means it *must* be one of our patients,' he muttered.

With a frustrated sigh he set it to one side. With her signature on the request form Leah would definitely know which patient it was. For all that she looked permanently exhausted, she took such a personal interest in each of their patients that she probably knew the details of every one of their current cases, right down to the name of the family pet. He would just have to ask her about it when she came in.

As if he'd conjured her up by thinking about her, Leah came in at that precise moment and she looked so white and strained that his guilt nearly buried him. The way she avoided looking at him made him more certain than ever that their problems all dated back to that night.

Remembering his decision to clear the air he cast about for a moment, trying to find a subtle way of bringing up the topic. He came up blank. It was so long since their conversation had covered anything other than work that he hadn't a clue how to start.

His eye fell on the mystery patient's results and, like a drowning man clutching at the nearest object, he seized on them as a way of starting some sort of communication going.

'Leah, what do you know about this?' he asked, lifting up the piece of paper.

She'd been about to settle herself at her desk but at

his words turned to approach him, as warily as a timid animal.

Silently cursing himself and afraid of scaring her away with a sudden move, he didn't move a muscle— at least, not intentionally. A certain part of his anatomy had other ideas as he slid his gaze over her elegant body and remembered...

He gritted his teeth when he saw how gingerly she took the piece of paper from him, obviously avoiding even the most accidental contact between the two of them, and knew he had an uphill climb in front of him if he was going to rebuild a good working relationship between them.

'We seem to have a phantom patient in the department,' he said, trying for a light-hearted approach. 'Stanley's sent through some results but I can't find her in the computer system. What do you know about Jane Smith?'

To his horror, what little colour she had in her face disappeared completely. For a moment she looked so ill that he was seriously concerned that she was going to keel over. He leapt up from his chair to look after her but when he reached out to take her arm he was shocked to have her flinch away from him as though even his touch was now abhorrent to her.

He was completely stunned by her reaction. Was this how bad it had become? Was she actually afraid of him now?

He felt sick at the thought. He would never raise a hand against her or any woman, no matter what the provocation. Surely she knew that much about him, even if she didn't like him any more.

The mystery patient was completely forgotten as he tried to find the words to reassure her. He couldn't promise not to touch her again. That would be totally impractical when the two of them worked together in an operating theatre. All he could do was promise her that any contact between them would be strictly work-orientated.

'Look, Leah, can you forget about those test results for a moment? I need to...' Where were the words when he wanted them? He'd never had a problem communicating before.

'Look,' he began again, his brain tangled in too many threads to be able to follow any of them properly, what with phantom patients, the desolate expression that had appeared in Leah's eyes and his need to clear the air between them. 'I'm sorry about what happened the other night... Well, not for what happened but the fact that it happened... Well, not even that, if I'm honest, but the fact that I've been like a bear with a sore head and avoiding you... Well, we've both been avoiding each other...' Oh, for heaven's sake! Why on earth was he rambling like this? He hadn't been this incoherent even when he'd been a tongue-tied teenager asking for his first date.

He snatched a steadying breath and forced himself to meet her eyes, suddenly struck by the fact that it almost looked as if she was about to cry. 'Leah, I promise you don't need to worry that I'll... What's the current term? Jump your bones? I promise that it won't happen again.'

He'd been right about the tears.

Even as he waited to see relief at his assurance, the first droplet fell, swiftly followed by a second and then a third.

'It's too late,' she whispered through trembling lips and turned the piece of paper she held so that it faced him. 'I'm pregnant.'

CHAPTER NINE

'WHAT do you mean, it's too late?'

David barely glanced at the lab result, more concerned with Leah's tears until she thrust the sheet towards him. Then he forced himself to read the words again and the bottom dropped out of his stomach.

Not again! a voice inside his head screamed, even as he was trying to come to terms with what she was telling him.

He could remember Ann saying exactly the same thing just a couple of weeks after he'd ended up in her bed in a moment of complete stupidity. She'd been beautiful and she'd been so flatteringly eager to be with him and had sworn that she was protected when he'd confessed that he wasn't in the habit of carrying condoms with him. Well, he'd been focusing so hard on his career that he'd had too little time to even *think* about having a social life, let alone commit himself to an intimate relationship.

He couldn't bear it, not if history really was going to repeat itself.

'You told me you couldn't get pregnant!' he accused, the betrayal gripping him in fierce talons and shredding the first green shoots of his growing trust. He wouldn't allow himself to remember the flash of guilty relief he'd felt when she'd told him that there was nothing stopping him from selfishly burying himself inside her body over and over again. Whether her inability to conceive was deliberate or a malfunction of her own reproductive system hadn't mattered in his desperation to forget the loss of the child he'd loved as his own.

'No, I didn't!' she argued fiercely, her knuckles white with tension as she crumpled the paper in her hand. 'I told you I couldn't have children, and we know better than most that it's not the same thing.'

'Well, however you want to split hairs, it was obviously a lie, if that result is to be believed.' He gestured towards the result sheet then rammed his fingers through his hair in disbelief. 'Dammit, what is it about me?' he demanded. 'Have I got ''sucker'' tattooed across my forehead or something?'

If he hadn't seen it happen, he wouldn't have believed how swiftly Leah's expression went from distraught to icy disdain.

With a single swipe of both hands she cleared all trace of her tears from her cheeks, then her chin tilted up and her shoulders went back.

'Don't worry about it, Mr ffrench. It's not your problem. Now, if you'll excuse me, I'd like to go home.' And without another word she strode swiftly out of the room and vanished from sight.

Leah had never been so glad that she used her car to get to the hospital. She'd barely held herself together long enough to shut the door before her tears began again, and they were still welling up in an inexhaustible supply when she finally locked herself into her flat.

The only thing she couldn't decide as she sobbed out her misery in the privacy of her bedroom was whether she was more unhappy about the unexpected pregnancy or about David's reaction to it.

Still, remembering his devastation about the loss of little Simon, any pleasure he might have felt at the prospect of another child had probably been overshadowed by memories of his double loss.

'Not that it would do him any good to get excited about it,' she murmured several hours later when she'd finally been able to control her immediate misery. At least her bonsai wouldn't take any notice of her swollen red eyes and blocked nose and they might even be able to help her reach some kind of equilibrium in advance of the misery still to come.

She tried to concentrate on repotting a young beech tree into a new pottery container, knowing that it would be difficult to empty her mind of the contempt she'd seen in David's eyes when he'd thought she'd tricked him. Even focusing on the exacting task of spreading the roots out so that they could support the tree's eventual height couldn't stop her remembering the reason why she'd begun raising bonsai in the first place, especially as she'd deliberately chosen a specimen from a different variety for each of the children she'd lost.

How *could* she forget when she would be choosing another one, sooner or later, to commemorate this latest doomed foetus?

The strident summons on her front doorbell was so unexpected that she nearly knocked the tree, pot and all, onto the floor of the balcony.

'Who on earth is that?' she muttered, not in the mood for company. With the level of security in this block of flats, any visitor should have been contacting her by the entry-phone at the entrance to the building, not at her own front door...unless they already had a key to the building.

With a sense of inevitability she brushed the loose soil off her hands and the front of her shirt and jeans and then walked towards the door with all the alacrity of a victim on the way to the gallows. Even though David usually stayed at the hospital much later than this, she didn't doubt for one minute that *he* was the one standing outside in their shared hallway.

'This is not going to be pleasant,' she whispered, with her hand hovering over the latch. At least she had to give him credit for the fact that it was going to take place out of earshot of their colleagues. Since she'd already been divorced before she'd moved to St Luke's, none of them knew about that part of her life.

She'd rather they didn't learn of her night of stupidity with David either, but that might become unavoidable if her condition…

Her train of thought was derailed by another peal of the bell, louder and longer than the last, and she resigned herself to the inevitable.

'Come in, David,' she invited quietly, already turning away as the door swung open with the sudden memory of her blotchy face. 'Can I offer you anything to drink?' A moment alone with a cold tap wouldn't do much, but…

'I don't need a drink, Leah. I need some answers,' he said, his voice much closer than she'd expected. Even so, his touch on her arm was unexpected as was its gentleness when he silently insisted that she turn and face him.

Just one glance at his beautiful eyes and the expression of concern in them was enough to have her fighting tears again. Even to the most casual observer it would be obvious that he was more worried about her now than angry…and she wasn't a casual observer.

'Sit down,' he said, leading her across to her settee and sitting down far too close to her for her peace of mind. If he was going to lambaste her again for misleading him, she needed him to be further away. How could she even think clearly let alone speak when she could breathe in the mixture of soap and man that was his alone, and could feel the warmth radiating from his body?

'First, I need to apologise,' he said abruptly and, as though wiped by the flick of a switch, her mind was clear.

'Apologise?' Just because her mind was working again, it didn't mean that she wasn't confused, especially when she'd expected his anger to have grown since she'd left him seething in the office.

'I tried to take advantage of my position as head of department to have a look at your medical records,' he admitted. 'Not that it did me much good.'

For a moment Leah didn't know whether she was annoyed that he'd tried or amused at his chagrin that he'd failed.

'It wouldn't,' she said wryly, easily able to see how much that had frustrated him. 'I left my records with my old obs and gyn department as the professor was the one who was treating me. I didn't move here until after my divorce and decided I wanted to come with a clean sheet. Donald was the only one who knew anything about my reproductive history.'

'So you only appear in St Luke's records as Jane Smith, patient of Dr Dawson?'

'Exactly. The last thing I wanted was for my private business to become public knowledge—not that Stanley would have breathed a word, of course. He's the soul of discretion. But somehow the hospital grape-vine…'

He nodded his understanding and was silent for a moment before he spoke again. 'They're going to find out sooner or later, you know. A pregnancy isn't some-thing you can keep secret for ever.'

'Not necessarily,' she whispered, having to force the words out through a rapidly tightening throat.

'You've already decided to have an abortion?' She couldn't tell whether he sounded shocked or dismayed and her eyes were too full of tears to see his face clearly enough to tell.

'An abortion won't be necessary,' she said bitterly, years of disappointment and despair forcing her to con-tinue. 'In seven attempts, I never even got to eight weeks before I lost the baby.'

'Oh, Leah,' he murmured, and suddenly, without knowing how it happened, she found herself cradled in his arms and sobbing her heart out on his shoulder.

It seemed like for ever before the tears finally abated and only the knowledge that she needed to tell him the rest of the story helped her to pull herself together. Even then, he wouldn't let her put any distance be-tween them and somehow she found it easier than she'd feared to talk with his arm wrapped securely around her.

'Start at the beginning,' he prompted when she hes-itated at the last minute, trying to decide where to be-gin the sorry tale. 'Were you married?'

'I was,' she confirmed, and it wasn't until she felt some of the tension leave his body that she realised that he hadn't been certain whether there had been another man in her life. If history had been repeating itself, he must have been afraid that he could lose this child, too. 'Ironically, we got married when I realised I was pregnant, just before finals. I lost the baby the day the results came out.'

Her story was no different than dozens of the women they saw, the special category who actually managed to conceive naturally over and over again, only to lose the baby before it had the slightest chance of survival. It was heartbreaking enough for those who discovered that their inability to conceive was due to a low sperm count or damaged Fallopian tubes or any one of the dozens of other combinations that prevented sperm and egg from meeting and combining to form that longed-for child.

For years she'd lived in that special hell where each time she became pregnant the baby stayed with her just long enough for her to know it was there and feel that precious protective connection before the onset of wrenching pain told her that it wasn't to be. And it hadn't mattered what tests the professor had per-formed. They'd never been able to find any reason why, or discover any treatment to stop it happening.

'In the end, Gordon got fed up with waiting for me to carry his son and heir and moved on to someone who could.' She knew there was little humour in her laughter; the ever-present pain wrapped tightly around her heart made it far closer to hysteria. 'Irony struck again—she had twins just four months after he left me, so he even managed to make up a bit of lost time. They were expecting their fourth the last time I heard.'

'I take it the two of you had all the tests,' he said and she could almost hear his brain switch into diag-nosis mode.

'With the prof as my head of department, what do you think?' she challenged, knowing that the man's reputation for thoroughness was legendary and world-wide. 'Just like the Whittiers, there was regular ovulation and a normal supply of sperm but, unlike them, the two elements actually got together, achieved fertilisation and went on to implantation. Mind you,' she mused aloud, remembering the months it had taken the two of them to get that far each time, 'it's never happened after just one night before.'

'Should I take that as a backhanded compliment?' he asked, and surprised her into an unexpected chuckle. She would never have believed she could find any part of this situation in the least bit funny. David had managed the impossible…in more ways than one. If only…

No. She wouldn't allow herself to wish for the moon. He might have managed to get her pregnant, but so had Gordon, over and over again. It was carrying the baby to term that was impossible.

'Anyway,' she said briskly, knowing their conversation had nearly run its course and just wanting to get the painful bit over and done with, 'I didn't know whether I was pregnant and even though I know that I'll lose it before I get to eight weeks, I know you had a right to know about it. I was just waiting for Stanley to let me know one way or the other and then I would have told you, but you saw the results first.'

The hot press of tears threatened to overflow and she really didn't want to start crying all over him again. The only thing she could latch on to in an attempt to control her shaky emotional control was her trees.

'I'll have to choose another tree,' she said, wondering which species would best commemorate David's child.

'Tree?' he echoed, sounding as though he was wondering whether she'd fallen out of one and landed on her head at some time.

'A bonsai,' she exclaimed, deliberately upbeat. She welcomed the chance to put a little distance between them as she got up to lead the way to her balcony even as she mourned the loss of his closeness. 'These are my babies now,' she said with a gesture towards the display she'd set up on slatted wooden shelving, glad that there was still just enough daylight for him to see them.

None of the seven trees was taller than knee-height and each was a perfect miniature, down to the smallest detail, of their cousins growing naturally in the countryside.

He was silent for a long moment while he looked at them one by one.

'You've grown these?' he murmured, and the admiration in his voice was balm for her soul. 'They're beautiful. Perfect.' He leant closer to touch a tiny leaf of the silver birch and she could see in his eyes the same fascination that had come over her with her first close encounter.

'Tell me about them,' he invited with a glance over his shoulder, and she knew it wasn't an idle request.

Pleased by his interest, she began by describing the tiny oak that had been her first choice, not knowing at the time that it was one of the more difficult species to develop a natural appearance in miniature form, given its habit of carrying the leaves in small bunches at the end of twigs. As ever, when she was thinking about the trees, her thoughts went to the babies they commemorated, and she barely realised until it was far too late to stop that she'd slipped into talking about the qualities of the trees—strength, resilience, grace, longevity—that she hoped her children would have shared...if they'd survived.

'Do they really help?' he asked with a touch of desperation in his voice as he straightened up and turned to face her, and she knew he was thinking of little Simon.

'To a certain extent, yes, because I can switch my thoughts off while I'm taking care of them.' She hated to destroy the glimmer of hope that appeared in his eyes, but it wouldn't be honest to tell less than the whole truth. 'But if you're asking if they can replace a lost child, then, no. Nothing can...ever.'

David wondered as he lay staring up at the ceiling in the darkness if Leah realised just how much those words had told him about her.

There had been a world of sadness and loss in them, but also a measure of anger at the cruel fate that had thwarted her so often.

She probably hadn't realised that, even as she'd wept at her impending loss, she'd had one hand spread protectively over the place where her child—*their* child—was nestled.

His heart had gone out to her in that moment. Any hint of anger at the fact that she'd told him less than the truth about her fertility had completely gone once he'd understood the reason.

He had seen this heartbreaking situation so many times in his work that it shouldn't have been able to affect him so strongly, but this time everything was different... What he couldn't work out was why. There were only two possibilities really. Either it was because the doomed child was his…this time, unequivocally his…or because it was Leah's child.

'But that raises other questions,' he murmured. Why should he care so much that Leah was going to go through such a devastating loss all over again? After all, he'd made a firm decision not to allow himself to become involved any more, so it couldn't be because he cared about her.

He snorted. 'And if you believe that…' he scoffed, silently admitting that, in spite of his determination, he *did* care about Leah. 'And not just as a colleague either,' he said aloud, feeling a measure of relief to hear the words spoken. He didn't know when she'd got under his skin—had it been that first day they'd met when she'd stood her ground so defiantly in the middle of a room full of chaos? He certainly wasn't ready to explore just how important she'd become to him, but that didn't mean he wouldn't move heaven and earth to do everything he could to spare her the heartache of another lost baby.

It would be a long shot, hoping he could succeed where others had failed especially as she'd spent years under the professor. He certainly wouldn't have left any stone unturned while Leah had been in his care, but how long ago had her last pregnancy been? Had the latest research about unexplained miscarriage emerged since then?

What was more to the point, how was he going to persuade her to let him do any tests? After seven miscarriages, she was clearly resigned to the prospect of losing this baby too. How was he going to find out if there was anything he could do to avert that without putting her emotions through a wringer all over again? He didn't want to raise her hopes, only to squash them.

Perhaps he should wait…not mention what he had
in mind until he saw her notes. He still had to get her
permission for that, and there was also the delicate
ethical position, with him as her departmental superior,
her one-time lover and the father of the child she carried. What would the hospital authorities think of the
fact that he also wanted to take on the role of her obs
and gyn specialist?

'But I can't pass her over to someone else!' he exclaimed, taking less than a second to dismiss every
possible candidate in the department. As good as his
young team was, the only other person to whom he
would entrust such a case would be Leah herself.

'No. *I'm* dealing with this. If there's the slightest
chance of saving her baby's life…' Even as he said
the words, a lightning bolt of realisation shocked him
into silence.

It wasn't just Leah's baby. It was his baby, too, and
the idea that it might not survive long enough to draw
its first breath suddenly terrified him.

He was finally drifting off to sleep when the shrilling of a distant telephone dragged him back to full
wakefulness.

He was already halfway across the room before he
realised that it wasn't even his phone ringing, but his
brain hadn't yet learned to ignore all the sounds from
the other flats.

'Not mine,' he muttered, while his pulse gradually
slowed towards a more normal rate, then it speeded up
again with the realisation that it was most likely Leah's
phone he'd heard.

With the thought that it was probably the hospital
ringing her to attend an emergency patient, all his pro-

tective instincts immediately leapt out from behind the concrete wall he'd erected around his feelings.

'If someone just wants a word with her, that's one thing, but if they're calling her back to the hospital...' He reached for his clothes, grabbing his off-duty jeans rather than bothering to find a suit at this time of night. 'If she's needed, then I'm going in, too,' he muttered, knowing he was being ridiculous but unable to quash the urge to keep an eye on her. Until he'd had a chance to talk to her and find out whether there was anything he could do to preserve their baby's life, he didn't want her put in any stressful situations.

The familiar sound of Leah's front door being unlocked told him he had guessed right and he stepped out of his door just seconds later.

'Shall I give you a lift?' he offered casually, with all the appearance of having been summoned to the hospital, too.

'Oh! Yes, thank you.' He'd startled her and she was endearingly flustered and still a little red-eyed after her emotional outpouring earlier that evening, but no less beautiful with her honey-coloured hair pulled back into a hasty ponytail and her grey eyes wide and soft. She nibbled her lip as they took the lift for speed and he imagined himself taking that plump flesh into his own mouth and...

Enough! he chastised himself silently, deliberately dragging his eyes away before his body's reaction became too obvious. *You haven't got time to go back for a cold shower.*

It's just my luck, he continued inside his head as she tucked her slender legs into the car with a smile of thanks. *My sex drive is all but invisible for years then I meet Leah and it appears with a vengeance.*

Knowing that his sex drive was the last thing he should be thinking about on his way in to St Luke's, even if he was sharing a car with Leah, he fought for some way to take his mind off the warm scent of a woman who had just climbed out of bed.

He couldn't talk about the patient they were going to see because he had no idea who it was. That just left his plan to persuade her to let him take another blood test, but perhaps that would be better if he waited until her notes arrived...*if* she gave her permission for him to request them from the professor.

There was only one way to find out, and he'd rather do it before they were surrounded by other members of staff.

'Will you be returning to the professor or are you happy for me to take care of you?' he asked, hoping he sounded as calm as if hers were no more complicated a case than that of any ordinary mother. She didn't need to know that his pulse rate was at least triple what it should be for a man of his age and state of health, and it was getting faster with each second that she made him wait for her answer.

'I suppose there's no real point in travelling all that way just for him to tell me that nothing's changed from the previous seven times,' she said eventually, her tone totally devoid of the happy lilt that her condition should have given her. It was every mother-to-be's right to feel excited about the miracle that was taking place inside her, and with everything inside him he wanted to be able to give that to Leah.

'Fine,' he said quietly, hoping his voice didn't betray his delight that he'd overcome the first hurdle so easily. 'I'll get you to sign the release form when we get to the office.'

'There's no hurry,' she said. 'It's not as if there's anything you can—'

'Leah, I won't be doing any less for you than I would for any other patient,' he said sharply. 'In fact, as my right-hand man...or woman, in your case...you should receive the best treatment the department can offer.'

'David, please...' As he parked the car in his assigned slot she struggled in silence for a moment before finding the words she wanted. 'In the circumstances, I really don't want a lot of fuss. I'd rather no one else in the department knew unless absolutely necessary.'

'If that's what you want,' he agreed, then had a brainwave of a suggestion that he was sure would instantly ease her tension. 'How about sticking to your Jane Smith alter ego for the time being?'

'Can I do that? Is it legal?' she demanded eagerly. 'I wasn't sure when I sent my sample up to Stanley whether I could end up being dismissed for...I don't know...falsifying an identity or something.'

'I haven't a clue,' he said as he released his seat belt. 'And I have no intention of finding out, so long as it's just the two of us in the know...'

'Thank you, David,' she said, with the first real smile he'd seen from her in far too long, a smile that dimmed all too quickly when she continued. 'It's not as if the deception will go on very long—another four to six weeks if previous episodes are anything to go on.'

'In the meantime, we have a patient waiting for us,' he said as he waved to Den on security duty and set off briskly for the bank of lifts. 'How much do you know?' he asked as the doors swept open to admit them, hoping that would prompt her into letting him know why she'd been called in at all.

'Nothing more than that Mrs Masson was making herself thoroughly objectionable, *again*, and upsetting the other mums and dads,' she said. 'Do you know any more than I do?'

The lift arrived at their floor and the noise that they could hear even before the doors opened was enough to make any evasive reply superfluous on his part.

'What on earth is going on here?' he demanded in an icy voice, barely needing to raise it to cut through the cacophony. 'You seem to have forgotten that this is a hospital. If you can't keep your voices down, I shall call Security and have everybody escorted out of the department.'

For just a second it worked like a charm, but he should have known that nothing could keep the objectionable Mrs Masson quiet for long. She seemed to have been determined to make their lives difficult from the first moment she'd arrived at St Luke's

'It's all very well threatening us, but what I'd like to know is where the two of you were while my babies are dying,' she demanded stridently. 'Why aren't you here doing the jobs you're paid to do?'

'Mrs Masson, I've warned you once,' David said coldly. It was difficult to keep control when he was suddenly furiously angry that the objectionable woman should have dared to attack his dedicated staff. As if Leah didn't have the right to her precious off-duty hours. She already worked horrendously long hours, and with an unexpected pregnancy of her own taking its emotional toll...

Enough! He couldn't afford to think about that, not

with a dozen or more pairs of eyes on him, waiting for him to resolve this unwelcome disturbance.

He fixed baleful eyes on the woman and gestured briefly along the corridor. 'If you have something you want to say to me, would you kindly join me in my office?'

Out of the corner of his eye he saw Sally grab Leah's arm and mutter furiously in her ear, but he couldn't stop to find out what that was about, not with Mrs Masson on his heels.

He'd barely got her settled and was preparing himself for the onslaught when Leah slipped quietly into the room and closed the door behind her.

Instantly, he felt better...calmer...as though a missing part of the picture had been replaced, although why he should feel all that just because Leah had joined them... He would have to think about that later.

'So, why are you letting *my* babies die?' Sylvia Masson demanded. 'Everyone else's are getting better, but mine...'

She broke off but in spite of the emotional tone of her words, David had the strangest feeling that there wasn't any real feeling for the babies in the accusation. But how could that be when—if their suspicions were correct—she'd perjured herself and risked her life to go through all the rigours of IVF to achieve the pregnancy? How could she not care desperately that the fact that she'd been implanted with triplets had significantly reduced the likelihood that any of the babies would survive?

'Mrs Masson, would you like me to call your husband?' Leah offered gently.

The angry woman turned to snap at Leah and David found himself tensing, ready to intervene, but then their eyes met, Leah's soft cool grey and Sylvia Masson's china-doll blue, and he saw a connection being formed although he didn't understand how or why.

Discretion kept him silent as the older woman's shoulders slumped in defeat, her attention all on Leah, now.

'You know, don't you?' she murmured, and gave a slightly hysterical laugh. 'It was probably obvious to everyone that I'm nothing more than mutton dressed up as lamb, trying desperately to hang on to the man I love when all he really wants is a son.'

Tears started to roll down her cheeks, eroding their way through the dark eye-liner to leave trails of despair.

'You *couldn't* understand,' she sobbed, grabbing the handful of paper tissues Leah offered as she rocked backwards and forwards in her misery. 'You've got your whole life ahead of you and I'm afraid he's going to leave me because I've already lost my son, and because you did the hysterectomy, I can't ever have another and…and my daughters will be dead any day now and then I'll be alone…all alone…'

'Shh, Mrs Masson…Sylvia…' Leah soothed, wrapping an arm round the woman's shoulders. 'I do understand.' She glanced up at David and he felt the connection sear the air between them as their gazes met. 'We *both* understand because we've both lost children and…and my husband left me to have a family with someone else.'

It was several minutes before the distraught woman could control her tears and a lot more than that before they could both reassure her that her two tiny daughters were having the best possible treatment during the roller-coaster ride of their fight for life.

'We're only minutes away,' David pointed out gently. 'Both of us live within sight of the hospital and even when we're off duty, the on-duty staff know we'll come in as soon as they call us—like we did tonight.'

Finally, Sylvia left to spend some time sitting between her daughters' high-tech cots and it was just the two of them in their shared office.

David was guiltily aware that he was probably taking advantage of the high emotions that had filled the room in the last hour, but he knew that he was unlikely to find a better opportunity to persuade Leah to agree to his request.

'Leah, before you leave…could I ask you to do something for me?'

'As long as it doesn't involve using my brain,' she said with a tired smile that made him feel guiltier than ever. 'The tension of that little encounter turned it to mush.'

'It's that little encounter that…well, partly anyway… But that woman's desperation to have a child…well…' Oh, for heaven's sake, he was making a complete hash of this. He'd never persuade her at this rate, so he might just as well… 'Will you let me do the tests?' he demanded bluntly, and when he saw her blink and take a step backwards he was certain he'd been too blunt.

But this meant so much to him. Far more than he'd ever believed it would, and the last time he'd lost a child it had nearly destroyed him.

'Tests?' she repeated warily. 'But, David, I've already told you that nothing does any good, so what use would double-checking what the professor has already—?'

'Humour me?' he begged with an attempt at a smile

that failed dismally. He was actually reduced to crossing his fingers in the secrecy of his pockets. 'If you think about it, this pregnancy is different to all the others because it's a different mix of genes, and if there's the slightest chance of a different outcome... Leah, I couldn't bear to lose another child just because I didn't do some blood tests.' Even as he was saying it he knew it was deplorable to play on her emotions that way, but if his suspicions proved correct...

'Oh, David. After seven failures for no apparent reason, we both *know* what's going to happen.'

She was refusing, he realised, feeling sick at his failure. Even after he'd shamelessly tugged on her heartstrings. Now he had nothing left in his armoury to persuade her, other than telling her his suspicions and raising her hopes unforgivably high.

If she *had* allowed him to do the blood test he wanted and he'd found that—as he suspected—her immune system was mistaking her pregnancies for an invader and sending in armies of NK cells to destroy them, he could have put her on powerful steroids to calm down her immune system enough for the baby to survive. Not the stilboestrol that had caused so many problems several decades ago when it had been used for a similar purpose but other—

'All right,' she said suddenly, interrupting his distracted thoughts and taking him completely by surprise. He was so jubilant that he almost missed her following words. 'But it has to be first thing tomorrow, before I have time to come to my senses, and on condition that this is strictly between the two of us.'

'And Jane Smith,' he added, hoping to end on a lighter note, but already he was filled with foreboding.

He could see that in spite of those seven lost pregnancies she was actually beginning to let herself hope.

Regret followed him like his own personal black cloud as he drove the two of them back to their flats.

He was almost certain that she hadn't already had her immune system investigated. Surely she would have mentioned it earlier when she'd been telling him about the tests she'd undergone, but he couldn't ask her directly without tipping his hand, and he didn't want to do that.

After all, what were the chances that he was guessing right? Was he just setting her up for more heartbreak? And, more importantly, what would it do to her if she lost another child after allowing herself to hope?

CHAPTER TEN

'COME on, Stanley. Ring me, now!' David muttered, his eyes fixed on the telephone while he waited for Leah's results.

He was desperately hoping they would come through before she returned to the office. At least then he would have a few minutes to assimilate the significance so that he could speak to her without his own emotions getting in the way.

He closed his eyes and shook his head, wondering where his detachment had gone. He'd been so determined that he wouldn't allow himself to get involved again, determined not to put himself through the agony of loving and losing. After a lifetime spent coping with his mother's suffocating love, he'd been wary about the very idea of marriage and family...until Ann had told him she was expecting his baby.

He'd honestly believed that when he'd lost Simon, something had died inside him...something that could never be revived.

'And what happened?' he muttered, hoping no one was out in the corridor listening to him talking to himself. 'Leah happened, that's what.'

Leah, the hard-working, talented, intuitive, compassionate, beautiful woman who made every molecule in his body sit up and take notice and had made his life a much brighter place. Leah, who was carrying the tiny foetus that—if his guess was right and the treatment worked—would become his son or daughter. Leah who in one night had gifted him with the most sensual and erotic memories of his life and who…was standing in front of him with a concerned frown on her face.

'Are you feeling all right, David?' she asked, and only someone who knew her well would have seen how tense she was under her calm exterior. Had she slept as little as he had after her decision to have the tests done? At least she'd had a morning of face-to-face appointments to occupy her mind after the sample had been delivered to the lab, while he'd sat here trying to concentrate on paperwork…and failing miserably.

'I'm fine,' he began, just as the phone rang. He pounced on it, desperate for the relief of hearing Stanley's voice on the other end. 'David ffrench,' he announced, and when it *was* Stanley, he found the tension only increased.

'Your guess was spot on,' the older man confirmed, bringing the hot threat of tears to his eyes. 'Jane Smith's system is reacting exactly as if it's rejecting an organ transplant, rather than to a pregnancy. I'll send the figures down with the rest of the batch, unless you want me to send it down straight away?'

'No hurry,' David said gruffly, only just remembering to thank the man for putting the test through as a priority before he fumbled putting the receiver back in the cradle.

'Was that Stanley?' Leah demanded with a mixture of dread and eagerness. She sank into the chair behind her desk as though her knees wouldn't hold her any more. 'What was the result?'

Unable to bear so much distance between them as he gave her the news, David came round to perch one hip on the corner of her desk then wondered if he'd done the right thing when her soft feminine scent twined distractingly around him. The pleading expression in her eyes brought him to his senses.

'While you were carrying Donald's work as well as your own, it might have slipped your notice that there's been some research going on for a couple of years now, trying to prove a link between an overreaction of a woman's immune system and repeated unexplained miscarriages,' he began as soberly as any medical school lecturer when what he really wanted to do was dance and sing that at least their baby now had a chance of life. 'Your tests showed that your white blood cell count is very high, similar to a patient with organ rejection after a transplant.'

The dawning comprehension on her face told him that he didn't need to explain that this could be a sign that her NK cells had been alerted to hunt out the foreign tissue inside her to kill it and get rid of it.

'What I propose is that we put you on steroids in the hope that it will damp your body's reaction down until the baby's well enough established to survive the rest of the pregnancy.'

'How long?' she demanded faintly, as though she was having trouble taking it all in. 'How far has the research gone? Have the researchers found a workable treatment protocol yet?'

'It's ongoing, but so far the optimum appears to be to the end of the first trimester, with a gradual withdrawal after that. They also suggest backing the steroids up with aspirin to prevent the NK cells from attacking the foetus through the blood-clotting mechanisms.'

It was heartbreaking to see the way she was teetering between disbelief and hope. David wished he could give her guarantees but...

'What's the success rate?' she whispered shakily, her thoughts obviously following a parallel route. 'Has the study been going on long enough for them to have any figures?'

'It's still very much in the experimental stage and relatively unproven, and the numbers are small, but so far it looks as if there's a twenty per cent success rate.' He knew he was playing devil's advocate, but he didn't want to get either of their hopes up too far.

'A one in five chance isn't very good odds,' she said soberly, then she took his breath away with a beatific smile. 'But it's so much better than no chance at all, David. So, when do I start taking the tablets?'

Three months had never gone so slowly, or been so exhausting, David thought with a heavy sigh.

In a way, it had felt as if he was holding his breath the whole time, and even now that Leah was coming off the steroids, David didn't feel that he could relax.

He should have been able to. After all, it looked as if the pregnancy was well established now, and in spite of her understandable caution, Leah was absolutely bubbling over with joy.

Especially today.

They'd deliberately come in to work early so that they could have the antenatal department to themselves. Feeling almost like giddy teenagers on a prank, they'd let themselves into the silent room that held the ultrasound equipment. She'd climbed up onto the table as he'd switched everything on, and as he'd run the probe over the gentle swell of her belly to reveal visible evidence that the baby was growing normally, his heart had swelled inside his chest and he'd wanted to crow from the rooftop.

It was a scary feeling after everything he'd gone through with Ann and Simon. He'd been so determined not to get involved, and it was only the fact that Leah's expression was similarly awed and fearful that made the whole thing bearable.

Except...

Except she was still determined to keep her condition a secret from their colleagues and she was definitely keeping him at arm's length, too. It was almost as if she felt she had to concentrate all her spare energy on the baby and had nothing left for even the most casual of social contacts. She certainly didn't seem to be willing to spend any time with him.

Even so, she seemed to have appreciated the cake he'd brought over to her flat to celebrate the fact that she'd finally managed to carry a baby past the heart-breaking eighth week. She'd clearly been touched that he'd even thought of it, but...

'Has she forgotten that it's my baby, too?' he demanded of the empty room, frustration at the limbo he'd been cast into finally exploding into words. 'Doesn't she realise that I'm every bit as concerned about the result of every test, terrified that something might go wrong?'

She'd certainly been terrified when she'd reached the end of the third month of the pregnancy and they'd started to wean her system off the steroids. She'd been convinced that it was too soon and that it would allow her immune system to turn on the baby and kill it.

Not that she'd said as much to him. She didn't say anything much at all to him and it was killing him, especially when he wanted to know everything—what she was thinking, what she was feeling… But to someone trained to observe, it had been easy to see the increased strain that gave a tense edge to her usually elegant movements, and as for the shadows around her eyes and the way she wouldn't meet his gaze…

'Dammit! She'll be halfway through the pregnancy soon,' he exclaimed, remembering his last glimpse of the curve of her belly before she'd pulled the loose top of her theatre scrubs down to hide the evidence, and the way his hands had itched to explore. 'That won't leave me long before the baby's born…'

The sound of the unfinished sentence hung in the air for a moment as the significance struck him. Leave him long enough for what? What *did* he want? What did he need to accomplish before the baby arrived? And why?

Before he could find any answers the phone interrupted his scrambled thoughts.

'David? I'm down in A and E,' Leah announced, overwhelming stress clear in her voice, and as his heart leapt straight into his mouth, he had all his answers.

How could he not have seen it before when it had been staring him in the face for weeks…months, probably?

All this time he'd been concerned on a professional level to try to ensure that Leah didn't lose her baby…*their* baby. He'd known how much it would hurt if he were to lose another child and could only imagine how devastating it would be for Leah.

What he hadn't realised until just this minute was that—baby or no baby—his life wouldn't be worth living if anything happened to Leah.

And she was at the other end of the phone, telling him she was in A and E.

Was she losing the baby? Haemorrhaging? Dying?

He couldn't lose her. Not now. Not before he'd held her in his arms again and told her that he loved her.

'I'm on my way, Leah. Hang on,' he said, cutting through her words and already half out of his seat, his heart trying to beat its way out of his chest.

Leah looked down at the blood and her heart rate doubled.

There was so much of it and it was so bright under the glare of the lights. Nobody could survive very long if they were losing blood at that rate, and everybody in the room knew it. They were running out of time and they couldn't afford to wait until David arrived. There was a baby at risk and that was all that mattered.

'He's on his way,' she said, although whether it was to let the rest of the team know or to reassure herself, she wasn't sure. She held her freshly gloved hands clear of contamination as she approached the patient, having to raise her voice to be heard over the cacophony of shrilling monitors. She didn't need all that noise to tell her that Ela Dahsani was in trouble. Under the natural golden hue of her skin she was already ashen with blood loss. 'We need to get on with it,' she muttered impatiently under her breath, waiting for the anaesthetist's nod before she could begin the emergency Caesarean.

'Please, Doctor, save my wife!' pleaded the distraught man clinging to her limp hand at the other side of the table, his dark eyes desperate in a face nearly as pale as the unconscious woman's. 'I nearly lost her when she had the cancer and we thought we would never be able to have this baby but…if you have to choose between the two of them, save my Ela!'

'She's under!' announced the anaesthetist. 'And her BP's already on the floor, so get moving!'

Even as she grasped the scalpel and prepared to make her incision, Leah knew how important it was to reassure the poor man.

'I'm going to do my best to save *both* of them, Arif,' she said firmly. 'So get ready for some sleepless nights when Ela makes you take your turn at walking the floor!'

Behind her, she heard the swing door slap open under a forceful hand and knew that David had arrived, but she was already preparing for the second stage of the incision, knowing that she didn't even have time to glance in his direction.

'Leah!' he exclaimed. 'What's going on? On the telephone you said—'

'You hung up before I could give you any details, but thanks for getting here so quickly... Suction! Oh, Lord, there's far too much blood,' she muttered under her breath, hoping Arif couldn't hear her. 'I think her uterus has ruptured. It's as thin as tissue paper...*wet* tissue paper!'

She reached a hand into the gaping incision and found the familiar shape of the baby's head then managed to hook a finger under a slippery little arm.

'Can you...?' She didn't even need to complete the sentence. David was already providing the steady pressure that would help her to lift the tiny being out of his dangerous abode.

'Clamp and scissors,' he offered, even as she supported the ominously limp form in both hands. She ached to do something to stimulate the baby into life but the paediatrician was ready at her elbow and Ela's life hung in the balance.

It didn't take more than a few seconds' examination and a sharing of professional glances with David to know what had to be done.

'Arif, we need to do an emergency hysterectomy if we're to have a chance of saving Ela. That means she'll never be able to have any more children. Do we have your permission?'

'Do whatever you have to!' he exclaimed, clearly overwhelmed by the speed of events. 'Just save my Ela!'

He'd barely spared his tiny son a glance, Leah marvelled as she and David worked as swiftly and as accurately as they'd ever done in the race against disaster. Even as they located the site of the haemorrhage and brought the blood loss under control, she was wondering what it would feel like to have a man love her that much.

She had no doubt that if all went well, Arif would be as loving a father as any child would want, but at the moment every atom of his being was concentrated on the woman he loved and willing her to stay with him. How could she herself do any less than her best to try to make it happen?

Even as she concentrated on her task, she was aware of a strange tension in David. It wasn't that he was any less proficient, but she now knew him well enough to know that there was definitely something else on his mind.

Something to do with her?

Probably, if it was anything to do with that last frowning glance he'd thrown in her direction before he'd left her to finish closing up their now stable patient. And in that case, it was something that needed sorting out, and the sooner the better.

*   *   *

Leah was about to shoulder her way out of the room, determined to track David down, when someone caught her sleeve.

'Will she *really* be all right?' pleaded the young woman who'd accosted her. 'Only I've never seen anyone lose that much blood before.'

For a moment Leah was taken aback, and it wasn't only by the young registrar's intensity. She'd only ever seen two people with eyes of that particular mixture of green and blue and as far as she knew, David and Maggie didn't have any other siblings or cousins.

'New to A and E?' she asked, even as she noted that the name on her tag was Libby Cornish.

'Painfully! Does it show?' she asked with a self-deprecating grin. 'How many of *those* am I going to be seeing in a day?'

'Hopefully, that's your quota for months!' Leah exclaimed. 'We really don't like performing emergency obs and gyn surgery in A and E. We'd rather take it at a more sedate pace up in our own department.' A department where she wanted to be *now*, confronting David ffrench with the fact that she was in love with him and...

Whoa! She was really getting ahead of herself here. She wasn't really going to put everything on the line like that. She wasn't brave enough to risk that sort of heartache again...or was she?

'I'm sorry, but I need to...' She gestured wordlessly towards the bank of lifts, then found herself adding, 'If you want to come up later and check on the Dahsanis, you're welcome.'

'Mr ffrench wouldn't mind?' she asked, almost eagerly, and Leah felt an unaccustomed twinge of possessiveness at the thought that the young woman was attracted to the man she loved.

'Not at all. He'd probably show you around the department himself, and spend the whole time trying to persuade you to change your specialty,' she joked, and made her farewells, suddenly eager to see David again.

'The Massons have disappeared,' Kelly Argent announced almost as soon as she arrived inside the department.

Leah stifled a groan, wondering how long it would be before she finally came face to face with David.

'What do you mean, disappeared?' she asked, trying to be patient. 'Have they gone back home?'

'That's just it!' the senior nurse exclaimed. 'This is the first time that we've actually had to phone them to come in—Sylvia Masson left late last night but both babies are very poorly again today and we thought they'd want to be here in case…' She didn't need to finish the thought. These tiny babies had such a fragile hold on life that their condition sometimes seemed to change every hour.

'Anyway,' Kelly continued, 'we've found out that they've been living in an hotel. Only they're not there any more. They've checked out without leaving a forwarding address.'

'How are the babies?' Leah asked as she turned towards the unit, taking the problem one step at a time and starting with the things that were marginally under her control. Tracking down parents was another thing entirely.

'They both looked very poorly when I started my shift—cranial bleeds,' she said sombrely. 'David's organising for an MRI to see how extensive the bleeds were, then we'll have a better idea how badly their brains have been damaged. Isn't it strange that both of them should have suffered at the same time…?'

A gasp somewhere behind Leah had them both twisting to face a shocked-looking Sylvia Masson.

'Are you talking about *my* babies?' she demanded faintly, reaching out one shaking hand to support herself against the wall. 'What's happened to them? They're not…?'

Leah and Kelly reached for her at the same moment, both thinking she was going to collapse.

'They're alive,' Kelly reassured her as Leah wrapped an arm around her and led her towards the unit, guessing that she would want to see for herself. 'Come and sit with them.'

For a moment the older woman held back, her expression torn as tears started to trickle down her pallid cheeks.

'I wasn't going to come back,' she whispered finally, confirming their suspicions. 'Marcus just wanted a son. He didn't want the girls, especially if they're going to be…brain damaged, and I didn't think I'd be able to cope by myself.'

'We don't know, yet, how much damage they've suffered. We'll have some idea after the scan, but we won't know for certain until—'

'It doesn't matter,' Sylvia interrupted fiercely, shaking off their supporting hold and suddenly straightening her shoulders. 'It doesn't matter if they can't… can't do all the things other children can do. They're *mine*. My precious babies. And however long they've got…whatever they can do…' She dashed her tears away and continued. 'I'm their mother and I'm

going to be there with them, fighting for them…
fighting with them…'

She turned and with a quiet sort of dignity made her
way to the sink to scrub her hands and don the required
protective clothing then sat herself in the seat she usually occupied, positioned between the two high-tech
cots that monitored her daughters' shaky condition.

Leah's eyes burned as she watched Sylvia put one
hand on each of the tiny babies, and although she
couldn't hear anything through the glass, she could see
Sylvia's lips moving and knew she was talking to
them.

'Well, that's another problem solved,' she murmured, halfway between joy and tears as she finally
made her way to the office she shared with David.
Now she just had to find some way of tracking the
man down and…

There he was!

She paused in the doorway, silent while she filled
her eyes with the sight of him and her heart swelled
with emotion. It was such a relief to be able to admit
that she loved him, if only to herself so far. And she
didn't only love his integrity and his commitment to
his work; she loved everything about him, including
those amazing eyes.

He wasn't working, for a change. His gaze was apparently fixed on something outside the window, but
from the expression on his face it was what was going
on inside his head that had all his attention.

Suddenly he raked his fingers through his hair and
groaned aloud before he caught sight of her and leapt
to his feet.

'David?' she said uncertainly as he strode towards
her, but it was the last thing she said before he swept

her into his arms and kicked the door closed behind her.

'Don't you *ever* do anything like that to me again!'
he groaned with his forehead pressed against hers.

'What?' she squeaked breathlessly as he tightened
his grip still further, almost as if he wanted to absorb
her into his body. Her toes barely reached the floor but
she didn't care. She'd never felt safer in her life.

'My blood ran cold when you rang from A and E,'
he said, the words sounding almost painful as he
forced them out. 'I thought you were losing the baby.'

The baby…?

Her heart sank. Was *that* what it was all about? Was
that why he'd had such a stony face and why he'd put
up such a barrier between them?

But what had she expected? He'd already lost one
child. Of course he'd be gutted if he thought that he
was losing another. She knew only too well what it
was like to cope with the possibility of loving and
losing a child again, even if she'd never actually held
one of her babies.

But if she was lucky this time…became part of a
set, mother and child…would that make it impossible
for him to accept…?

'Then…' he grated, dragging her out of her despair-
ing thoughts with a hand cradling each side of her face,
tilting it up until her eyes met his. That blue-green
gaze was so intent that there was no way she could
mistake his sincerity, even as her heart stumbled with
uncertainty. 'Then I realised that *you* matter more to
me than the fear of losing a baby…

'Oh, don't get me wrong,' he continued hastily
when she tried to interrupt. 'I know it would have bro-

ken your heart if *you* had been the patient down in A
and E and it was *your* baby that…'

'Me?' she questioned, momentarily silencing him
with one set of fingertips across his mouth while her
heart stuttered and leapt with dawning joy. '*I* matter
more than…' Her other hand caressed the soft swell
of her growing child.

'Yes, *you*.' He covered her hand with one of his
own. 'That's not to say that I don't want this little
person, because I do…in spite of…'

'In spite of the fact that you're afraid of something
going wrong?' she challenged when he faltered, suddenly determined to get everything out in the open.
There was no chance of any sort of lasting relationship
between them if they didn't.

'In spite of the fact that I was absolutely determined
not to let anyone get close to me, because I knew I
wouldn't survive that sort of pain again,' he admitted
quietly. 'I thought we could have a purely professional
relationship until that night. Even then I tried to stay
away from you, but I should have known I was
wasting my time. As soon as I met you, life
seemed…brighter. I felt more…hopeful…more opti-
mistic than I had since I lost Simon. Dammit, woman!'
he exclaimed. 'I fell in love with you and you seemed
ideal for me—a career woman who couldn't have children.'

'Then I found out I was pregnant…'

'And I panicked,' he admitted grimly. 'But even
while I was scared to death that history was going to
repeat itself, I was slowly coming to realise that I
didn't just want a cordial professional relationship with
you. If I'm honest, that would never have been enough
for me either.'

'And now?' The joy dawning inside her was almost too much for her to contain.

'Now I know exactly what I want,' he declared. 'I want it all—you, the baby and the whole story-book happily-ever-after…if you'll have me?'

'What are you suggesting? That we move in together for the sake of the baby—so you can be there while he or she is growing up?' She didn't want to be presumptuous. If that was all he was offering, she'd take it, even though she wanted so much more. But he'd married once for the sake of a baby and he wouldn't necessarily want to…

'What do you think I'm suggesting?' Suddenly he dropped to one knee in front of her, one hand held tightly in his as he looked up at her. 'I'll say it in words of one syllable so that there's no confusion. Leah, I love you and the unexpected miracle we managed to create. Will you do me the honour of becoming my wife?'

'Your *wife*?' she whispered in disbelief, and with the realisation that everything she'd ever wanted was within her grasp, her knees refused to hold her any longer. 'Oh, David, yes! I'd love to be your wife. I love you,' she said, and threw her arms around him as they knelt together on the floor.

His mouth went from gentle to hot and hungry in an instant and she responded as she had that night— passionately, with her own hunger leaping up to meet his.

It was several minutes before either of them realised that someone was knocking on the door and at least that long before they were on their feet and calm enough to be able to invite their visitor in.

'I'm sorry. Is this an inconvenient time?' Libby

Cornish asked when she stuck her head around the door. 'Dr Dawson said I could come up to see the Dahsanis' baby.'

For a moment, Leah didn't dare look at David or she knew she would have laughed aloud. If the young registrar with the beautiful blue-green eyes had knocked a couple of minutes earlier she would have interrupted David's proposal, and a couple of minutes later…

'It's not inconvenient at all,' David said, and looked down at Leah with a smile that showed her she'd finally banished the last of the shadows in his eyes. 'In fact, you can be the first to congratulate me. Dr Dawson…Leah…has just agreed to marry me.'

0805/03a

MILLS & BOON®

Live the emotion

_Medical
romance™

THE DOCTOR'S SECRET SON
by Laura MacDonald

When Luke left the country, he left Ellie's life. The
distance between them made it easier for her
not to tell him she was pregnant with his child. It
also made it easier to cope with her heartbreak.
Suddenly, he's back – and working at her practice!

A NURSE' S SEARCH AND RESCUE
by Alison Roberts

Tori Preston loves her new career in Urban Search
and Rescue – and she's enjoying the company of her
mentor, Matt Buchanan. But Matt is raising four
nieces and nephews alone – and Tori's not looking
for any new responsibilities…

THE FOREVER ASSIGNMENT by Jennifer Taylor
(Worlds Together)

Now that Kasey Harris is part of the team, the
Worlds Together aid unit is ready for its assignment.
But head of the team is gorgeous surgeon Adam
Chandler – and he and Kasey have met before…

Don't miss out!
On sale 2nd September 2005

*Available at most branches of WHSmith, Tesco, ASDA,
Borders, Eason, Sainsbury's and most bookshops*

Visit www.millsandboon.co.uk

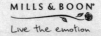

MILLS & BOON®

0805/03b

Live the emotion

_MedicaL
romance™

THE ITALIAN SURGEON by Meredith Webber

(Jimmie's Children's Unit)

All eyes are on the newest member of the team at Jimmie's – tall, dark and handsome Italian surgeon Luca Cavaletti. Luca only has eyes for Dr Rachel Lerini. The closer Luca gets, the more she runs away – but he is determined to make her smile again – and even love again…

HER PROTECTOR IN ER by Melanie Milburne

(24:7)

Five unexpected deaths have brought hot-shot city detective Liam Darcy to town. Dr Keiva Truscott is first on his list of suspects. All Liam's instincts tell him she's innocent – but until the case is closed he can't possibly fall in love with his prime suspect…!

THE FLIGHT DOCTOR'S EMERGENCY
by Laura Iding   *(Air Rescue)*

Flight Nurse Kate Lawrence has learned through hard experience that laughter is the best healer – and it looks like Flight Doctor Ethan Weber could use a dose of it himself. The single father's lifestyle is all work and no play – something Kate is determined to change.

Don't miss out!
On sale 2nd September 2005

Available at most branches of WHSmith, Tesco, ASDA, Borders, Eason, Sainsbury's and most bookshops

Visit www.millsandboon.co.uk

FREE

4 BOOKS AND A SURPRISE GIFT!

We would like to take this opportunity to thank you for reading this Mills & Boon® book by offering you the chance to take FOUR more specially selected titles from the Medical Romance™ series absolutely FREE! We're also making this offer to introduce you to the benefits of the Reader Service™—

- ★ **FREE home delivery**
- ★ **FREE gifts and competitions**
- ★ **FREE monthly Newsletter**
- ★ **Books available before they're in the shops**
- ★ **Exclusive Reader Service offers**

Accepting these FREE books and gift places you under no obligation to buy; you may cancel at any time, even after receiving your free shipment. Simply complete your details below and return the entire page to the address below. You don't even need a stamp!

YES! Please send me 4 free Medical Romance books and a surprise gift. I understand that unless you hear from me, I will receive 6 superb new titles every month for just £2.75 each, postage and packing free. I am under no obligation to purchase any books and may cancel my subscription at any time. The free books and gift will be mine to keep in any case.

M5ZEE

Ms/Mrs/Miss/Mr...Initials ....
BLOCK CAPITALS PLEASE

Surname ....

Address ....

....

....Postcode ....

Send this whole page to:

The Reader Service, FREEPOST CN81, Croydon, CR9 3WZ